THE PICTURE OF DULCE GARCIA

GARCIA

The Coven Book 1

ALANA ALBERTSON

Bolero Books

The Picture of Dulce Garcia
Copyright © 2017 by Alana Albertson
Cover design by Regina Wamba of MaeIDesign.com
Cover Photography: Regina Wamba of MaeIDesign.com

Bolero Books, LLC
11956 Bernardo Plaza Dr. #510
San Diego, CA 92128
www.bolerobooks.com

All rights reserved.

✿ Created with Vellum

The Picture of Dulce Garcia

The Coven—Book 1

The perfect picture.

Amazing airbrushing and a flattering filter, and I look like the starlet I've always wanted to be.

You know, one of those perfect Instagram models with a million followers.

Like one of the girls that Sebastian would date.

So, I utter a foolish wish. If only I could look like my picture forever.

But forever is a long time. And some wishes can't be broken.

The price of vanity is high.

And my mad wish may cost me my soul.

AWARDS

The Picture of Dulce Garcia

1st Place Editor's Choice Award SDSU Writer's Conference 2015

2nd Place Young Adult Category RWA Melody of Love Contest 2015

3rd Place Young Adult Category of the 2011 RWA Stiletto Contest

3rd Place Young Adult Category of the 2011 RWA Launching A Star Contest

3rd Place Young Adult Category of the 2011 RWA Heart of the Rockies Contest

PROLOGUE

DORIAN GRAY

A mist washes over my face, and I'm jolted from my slumber in my Paris apartment. I peer out at the Abbey of Saint-Germain-des-Prés; the eerie quiet of the morning contrasts with the rumbling in my heart.

It has happened.

My blood burns and my pulse quickens. I sense her presence somewhere in the world. Where is she? More importantly, who is she?

Over one hundred years. Alone. On my own. With no one by my side. Lord, I sound like that melancholy song from that dreadful adaptation of Victor Hugo's *Les Misérables*. Oscar Wilde spoke of that miserable bastard; they'd been friends in Paris in the late eighteen-hundreds. I was just a young lad back then before Basil painted me. Before I became immortal. Before I'd given Oscar my story to write.

"How sad it is! I shall grow old, and horrible, and dreadful. But this picture will remain always young. It will never be older than this particular day of

June... If it were only the other way! If it were I who was to be always young, and the picture that was to grow old! For that—for that—I would give everything! Yes, there is nothing in the whole world I would not give! I would give my soul for that!"

Those foolish words ruined my life over one hundred years ago. A wish made to the painter of my portrait has trapped me in ever-lasting youth and damned me to eternal hell. My lovers have grown old and left me, and I'm forced to survive in a modern world that I don't understand. Opera, ballet, and literature have been replaced by rap, hip-hop and eBooks. My heart is old, yet my body is young. And I have no one to share my life with.

Has someone now befallen my curse?

This sense. This primordial feeling yelling at me to find her.

When I heard that Oscar was on his deathbed, I'd visited him in Paris. He was ill with meningitis, and I was ill from loneliness. I wanted to die with him; I begged him to help me end it. To slash my picture as he had written in his book because I didn't have the emotional strength to do it myself.

But instead, Oscar told me, "One day, Dorian, one day you will no longer be alone. Another vain soul will succumb to your curse. And you will finally live a full life. I will be long gone, but you, dear Dorian, will live forever."

I creep out of my bed, careful not to wake the naked girl by my side. I grasp my phone and click on the News Daily site. Any news in the world is always posted there. Despite my reminiscing about the joys of the past, I do love modern technology.

My finger slides down the screen. And once I see her picture, I know.

Dulce Garcia.

Golden tinged eyes, pouty lips, silky black hair.

A beautiful young starlet from America. She'd passed out and hit her head in her television trailer after a night shoot and has been in a coma for two weeks. Rumors echo through Hollywood that she's had extensive plastic surgery. A production assistant is quoted saying that she, "looked exactly like an airbrushed cover of a magazine" after her night filming.

But I know the truth.

She is just like me. In a moment, in a flash, she must've made a foolish wish. Words that can't be taken back. Words that will change her life forever.

Unlike me, she won't have to go through it all alone.

I'll travel around the world to find her, claim her as mine for eternity. I'll showered her with jewels, art, anything her heart desires. I'll fill her nights with never-ending ecstasy.

She owes me nothing—but her soul.

"The only way to get rid of a temptation is to yield to it."

THE BOOK

*One hardly knew at times whether one was reading the spiritual ecstasies of some mediaeval saint or the morbid confessions of a modern sinner. It was a poisonous **book**. The heavy odour of incense seemed to cling about its pages and to trouble the brain. The mere cadence of the sentences, the subtle monotony of their music, so full as it was of complex refrains and movements elaborately repeated, produced in the mind of the lad, as he passed from chapter to chapter, a form of reverie, a malady of dreaming, that made him unconscious of the falling day and creeping shadows.*

— OSCAR WILDE, THE PICTURE OF DORIAN GRAY

My eyes focus on the airbrushed, filtered picture of myself that *Teen Glam* magazine just uploaded on their Instagram. Is this really me? How did they make me look so hot? As I zoom in to get a closer look at the image, my bracelet hooks on the straw of my coconut milk iced Mexican mocha, and I spill it all over my brand new, red velvet corset.

"*¡Ay, Dios mío!*" I jump up and swipe a damp towel from Eva's makeup cart, but the tan liquid soaks in too fast. "If Mr. Mulberg sees this stain, he'll freak. Like he needs another reason not to renew my contract."

"You're the one who's freaking." Eva sets down my lipstick, steals the towel from my hand, and helps me wipe the mess off my chest. "I don't care that you have night shoots—you're too young to be drinking that stuff, anyway."

"I'm not too young. I can't live without the bitter chocolate caffeine rush." I see a dark spot on the seam. "There's more right there—"

"Stop." She swats my hand out of the way and keeps blotting. "You need to calm down, Dulce. Mr. Mulberg was just trying to scare you when he threatened to fire you. There's no way this series could go on without one of the members of the coven. The executive producer of a hit series wouldn't dare break up the pack. Unless you do something crazy, like get pregnant."

Well, there isn't a chance of that happening. I'm a virgin. And the boy I'm in love with acts has parked me in the friend zone. "He is *too* looking for a way to replace me. I turn seventeen in a month! That's like forty in Savvy Network years." I grab the towel back and scrub frantically. "Just last week, he caught me sipping a peach dream smoothie and called me into his office to tell me to stop drinking out of the straw because I will get lines around my mouth. And he's right! Look at this!" I point to a suspicious looking smile line on my face. "Do you see these big craters on my cheeks? He'll probably make me get Botox! No, stop rolling your eyes—costuming already does its best to flatten me out."

I swear, I can recite Mr. Mulberg in my sleep. "Tween witches *do not* have breasts." We're only supposed to be fourteen on the show. That's why he makes us wear these boned corsets, so we look like we haven't hit puberty. "He's going to take me into his office and say, 'Dulce, Savvy stars do not get coffee stains on five hundred dollar corsets from costuming, not if they like their jobs.' I'm totally doomed."

"Honey, you're crazy." She points to the custom Otomi fabric sofa I've somehow managed to squeeze inside my dressing trailer, and, like a good dog, I sit. I spend so much time in here that I had to spruce it up. There are two Mexican-style altars on my desk that I made for *Dia de los Muertos:* one for my mom and one for my dad. A poster of my favorite film noir movie *Gilda* hangs in the corner. A bouquet of honey-colored marigolds, white mums, and flame-colored gladiolas, which I picked myself, are in a Talavera vase on the small table by the door. I had to do *something* to make it seem like a real room.

"You're gorgeous, and you don't look a day over thirteen. Just wait until you're my age," Eva says. "Then you can complain about wrinkles, cellulite, and thinning lips."

Man, everyone who works in the entertainment industry is so messed up. Eva is only twenty-five years old, and just like me, she thinks she looks ancient. I lean back on the sofa as she aims a blow dryer at the stain. She's been my personal makeup artist all three seasons of *The Coven,* and I completely adore her, but she just doesn't get it. It isn't her fault, though. She works *behind* the cameras, and from there, things look totally different than how I see them. Being in front of the camera makes everything more intense. More live or die. More ... well, crazy.

My eyes dart back to the photo on my phone that has caused this mess in the first place. It isn't just any snapshot. No, it's a full-screen portrait with the headline, "Dulce Garcia—The Hottest Teen in America." Hardly. I am so not your typical Savvy Network starlet. I'm not blonde or perky or happy. Certainly not an Instagram beauty. That's the last thing I ever expected to see. My publicist must've paid a pretty penny to get them to feature me. My team is doing everything they can to keep my name in the press because my contract renewal is up.

But somehow, in that picture, I look amazing. I've been airbrushed before but nothing like this—it doesn't even look like me. There is no trace of the bump on my nose. My skin is almost glowing, and my acne has vanished. My brown eyes look like they have flecks of gold in them, which they totally don't. My lips are plump and pouty. And my hair—wow, that photo has me looking almost glam with long, black hair that is perfectly straight and frizz-free. Like a teenage Wonder Woman who's super skinny with plump breasts, not the B-cups I currently rock. Who had they hired to double as me? *I* certainly never look like that. Maybe they merged my photo with another star's picture? I didn't know airbrushing could make me look like another person.

I close my eyes and imagine how easy my life would be if only I looked like that forever. Not only would Mr. Mulberg renew my contract for sure, but I'd also never have to sit through hair or makeup again nor would I have to go to the gym every day.

Unfortunately, as good as the picture is, it doesn't resemble me at all, which pisses me off. I don't want my fans to think I'm this boney chick with fake breasts and perfect hair.

I wonder if Sebastian has seen it.

Eva sees the picture on my phone. "Oh, they sent over an advance copy of the magazine." She points to a lone copy that was hidden behind her chair.

I pick up the magazine, my hands tracing the cover. "I can't believe how hot I look!"

She finally puts down the blow dryer and resumes placing red and black rhinestones around my eyes. "Yeah, I saw it. Nice. Sometimes I forget what you look like for real—I'm so used to painting you up like Ria." She strikes the pose of my gothy witch from the series poster. She makes the pouty face just right. It's nothing like the smile in this shot.

"Seriously? That's not what I really look like. What did they do with the zits? Where's my cowlick? I *never* look like this. I'm not a troll or anything, but I'm no Victoria's Secret Angel."

"You're definitely not a troll, though you did make an adorable gnome in that fantasy episode last month."

She waits for a laugh, but I give her nothing.

"Stop squirming. You're a teenager. Of course, that picture is airbrushed. But you look better in person. You're beautiful."

No, I'm not. "I'd do anything to look like this picture. Anything. I'd sell my soul."

A flash of light passes before my eyes, momentarily blinding me.

Eva's mouth drops, and she grasps me on both sides of my head, leans down, so we are eye to eye, and glares at me. "You're crazy! Don't ever say that you would sell your soul. Go say some Hail Marys or whatever it is that you Catholics do."

The aura in my head stops, and I slink down into my chair. "I'm just kidding, Eva. Relax."

"Maybe . . . but I believe in that evil possession stuff. Like someone is always watching, listening, and waiting to lead the souls of the weak into eternal damnation." She gives a long, labored sigh. "Now, quit looking down, unless you want to be right about getting fired. If Mr. Mulberg sees these zits"—she points to the mirror—"*that's* how you'll be looking all the time, and I'll be painting someone else up as Witchie-poo every night. Now hold *still*."

Eva finishes putting on my war paint and bids me goodbye. I look in the mirror and don't recognize myself. We're shooting a *Dia de los Muertos* episode even though the real holiday is a month away. I love the makeup—alabaster painted skin, heavy black eyeshadow, long eyelashes, and a cool spider web motif on my forehead and lips.

I thumb through the script for the night shoot. The writers have added some altars, marigolds, and gothy makeup—they must think that Latino décor alone is sufficient to honor this celebration. They clearly haven't researched the holiday, which happens to land on my birthday. It is my favorite, especially because my mom died giving birth to me and my father died serving as a Marine in Iraq. *Dia de los Muertos* is about honoring our dearly departed loved ones. The one time a year their spirits can visit us from the underworld, the land of the dead.

But unfortunately, there is no scene about honoring the dead. Tonight, my coven will simply perform a spell for everlasting youth. A Wiccan spell which has nothing to do at all with Day of the Dead, but clearly *The Coven* writers don't have a clue about my culture. Even so, the Wiccan spell is badass. If only these spells really worked as they did on the show. It's not as if I want to be sixteen forever, but I'm also not ready to age out of this job. There's no guarantee I'll get something else after this gig. I'm an orphan—I need this money. I often wonder what it would be like to have a close-knit family. A sister to confide in, a brother to protect me, a mother to comfort me, and a father to adore me. Sometimes I fantasize about family camping trips and board games around the fire. At least I have my bestie, Halia. My aunt is my legal guardian, but sometimes I wonder if she loves me or my paycheck.

I toss the script aside. Same circle casting, same call to quarters, same goddess invocation. One pass is all I need to get the scene down. My brain calls for something with more meat. I reach into my bag and take out this awesome book that my tutor, Yvonne, gave me last month.

Anthology of 19ᵗʰ Century Literature of the Supernatural and Science Fiction. The embossed cover is a gorgeous sunflower color and even has a creepy dedication written in cool Gothic letters. *"An artist should create beautiful things but should put nothing of his own life into them."* Yvonne probably wrote that herself. She told me that some creepy old man named Henry had given her the book at Paris's Père Lachaise Cemetery immediately after she kissed Oscar Wilde's tomb.

Yvonne could've skipped the crazy burial ground story, and I still would have loved it. This book rocks—vampires, invisible men, monsters, haunted pictures, alternate personalities, werewolves, special potions, mummies, zombies, ghosts. If only they would pay me to do *that* stuff in the show, then I'd be stoked. I'm obsessed with

Gothic fiction and wish I could read all day. Acting isn't all glam and fun like everyone thinks—not by half, and certainly not with Mulberg's scripts. It's not like I can quit to go find something more appealing. In the back of my mind, I keep thinking that maybe I'll be able to squirrel away enough of my own money, so I'll never have to work again. Maybe then I can get into Harvard and study literature. I know I'm blessed, and millions of girls would love to be on a hit television show, but deep down I just want to be a normal teen and not have to worry that every mistake I make will end up on the cover of a tabloid.

A production assistant opens the creaky trailer door. "Dulce, we need to leave for your scene in five minutes." She turns to leave but then catches the door right before it swings closed. "Oh, and don't forget to bring *The Book of Shadows*. And Winter, too." The door slams shut before I can answer her.

I blow out a deep breath, my cheeks puffing with the effort. Right. My soft, blue-eyed, white bunny, Winter, is my witch's familiar on the show. All the other girls leave their animals on set after filming, but I just fell in love with Winter, and I can't bear to abandon him in a cold, dank stage cage. So, I take him home with me every night. I walk over to Winter's exercise pen, but he's missing. I open the fridge and throw some cilantro and strawberries down—he'll be out in a minute for sure.

Now, where is that darn book? I accidentally brought it home last night.

Stupid prop.

It's supposed to be a real Wiccan text that contains cool rituals, but the set version just has the made-up spells we use on the show and other notes for our scene.

I rummage through my bag but can't find *The Book of Shadows* anywhere. "C'mon, c'mon . . ." I mutter. I'm sure I didn't leave it at home when I practiced the spell. It has to be here somewhere. Seriously, it *has* to be. I tear apart my trailer. "Where the . . .?" If I lose that thing, Mr. Mulberg will fire me for sure.

"Dulce, NOW!" barks the assistant.

Totally panicking, I dump the contents of my bag on the ground. *The Book of Shadows* cover jacket floats out and lands perfectly on the top of my anthology—but just the jacket. I took it off yesterday so I wouldn't get it dirty. Then I hear some crunching—and get an awful feeling in the pit of my stomach.

"Oh, please, Winter, tell me you're not eating—" But even as I turn, I know what I'll find. "Winter, no!" My rabbit is munching through *The Book of Shadows!*

I swipe the book from him, but it's too late. It's toast.

"Oh, man. Winter, what have you done to me?" I'm a dead witch. I might as well bathe in my boiling cauldron.

Desperate, I grab the dust cover before Winter can get his little teeth on it and scoop up my anthology. My whole body seems to sigh in relief when the cover slips seamlessly around the collection of novels.

Crisis averted! The director will never know the difference. Like he ever looks at a prop up close. Luckily in tonight's episode, I'm the only one reading from *The Book of Shadows,* so my fellow witches will be clueless as well.

I can't bear to leave my magazine picture behind. Maybe I can show it to Sebastian? I fold the cover of the magazine and place it in the book. Then for good luck, I pause and decide to say a quick blessing that I've memorized—not that hard because it is my opening voice-over at the start of each show's credits. I place the book on my *Dia de los Muertos* altar and begin the dedication.

"Bless this Book in the name of the goddess and the god.

Who guide my feet on the Path of Beauty.

Let it be filled with wisdom and knowledge.

Let me use it only for good.

Let me share it with those who need it."

That should do it. My plan will work, I know it will.

I tuck my newly anointed *The Book of Shadows* under my arm, scoop up my naughty bunny, and shove him in his cage. Thirty seconds later, I'm sitting in the little golf cart and being whisked away to the set.

THE WISH

*He had uttered a mad **wish** that he himself might remain young, and the portrait grow old; that his own beauty might be untarnished, and the face on the canvas bear the burden of his passions and his sins; that the painted image might be seared with the lines of suffering and thought, and that he might keep all the delicate bloom and loveliness of his then just conscious boyhood.*

— OSCAR WILDE, THE PICTURE OF DORIAN GRAY

CHAPTER 2

Our show films in Marin, on the *other* side of the Golden Gate Bridge. Most scenes are shot on location at Redwood High School in Larkspur or on a sound stage in downtown San Rafael, but for the ritual scenes, we shoot at various locations around beautiful Marin County. For this spell, the girls and I are filming at the peak of Mt. Tamalpais. As the driver and I journey up the hill, I'm grateful to be out here in nature away from the Hollywood scene. The wind is blowing, and I can only see the moonlight amongst the clouds and fog. But as we get to the ridge, we break through the fog bank. It's like fifty-five degrees and still as death up there on top of the world.

But my beautiful view is unfortunately obstructed with production equipment. There are lights and deflectors, camera operators adjusting angles, lighting guys flipping switches, and key grips pushing everything every which way. So much for leaving Hollywood behind.

I hand Winter to our animal trainer, and she corrals him into his animal pen next to the cages of the other familiars—an iguana, a chinchilla, a prairie dog, and a raven. No cats though—Mr. Mulberg thinks they're way too stereotypical.

Sebastian is lingering on the set, even though his scene wrapped earlier this afternoon. He's dressed like a dead mariachi, complete with sexy tight pants. I try not to stare at his butt, but I have no self-control.

"Hey, Duls." He walks over to me and gives me a big hug. His red embroidered *corbatin* rubs against my neck, my skin itches from the cheap fabric. "I saw your picture. It's nice, but it looks nothing like you."

I bite my nails and gaze into his brown eyes. Man, when did he become so sexy? "I know. They made me look totally hot."

His jet-black hair skims his forehead. He keeps his pace with mine as I hurry over to my angry costars. "Nah, babe, that's not what I mean." He sheepishly glances down at his boots, and all I can see are his long eyelashes. "You don't need all that makeup. You look better just normal, just nothing but you."

My lips break into an involuntary grin, but I remind myself that he's a total flirt and isn't even remotely interested in me.

Well, I think he isn't. I don't really know. I've wanted him forever and ever, but I've never thought I had a chance. I've always taken myself out of the game.

Even so, his words give me false hope. I want to ditch the shoot and talk to him, but that's completely out of the question. "I'm totally late, but I'll see you tomorrow. Just got the script. Looking forward to our kiss," I tease.

He leans into me and whispers into my ear, "Let's get together early and practice."

I want him to kiss me then and there, but I decide to play it cool.

He's just playing with me. Sebastian's gorgeous, and he can have his pick of any girl in and out of Tinseltown. But he has never chosen me.

Since we always hang out off set and play boyfriend and girlfriend on the show, all the tabloids swear up and down that we're hot and heavy. It's not the truth. I fantasize about being with him, but I can never tell if he's just being flirty, or he really wants to go out with me. And we aren't like other teens—if we hook up and it doesn't work out, we won't just be able to defriend each other on Facebook and stop following each other's Instagrams. Our publicists would have to issue public statements, and we would still have to see each other every day, which would no doubt be awkward. So, until I'm sure he totally wants to get serious, I refuse to go there.

I give him a quick peck on the cheek. "Gotta go. I'll see you later."

He hugs me a tad too long, and I inhale his scent. He finally releases me and then heads off to his golf cart.

I run over to the other girls. They're huddled together—clearly freezing—under a towering Douglas fir. For this episode, we're all costumed in brightly colored Mexican-style peasant dresses with flower garlands woven into our hair. Sometimes I think we look more like a multi-ethnic girl pop band than a coven of witches, which isn't by accident. We'd all been cast to pander to the diversity demographics—I'm Latina, Halia is Hawaiian, Marcilla is Russian, Vikki is Haitian, and Asha is Egyptian.

As I approach the clan, Marcilla and Vikki give me dirty looks, and Asha doesn't even bother to acknowledge my presence.

Halia comes over and wraps me in a hug. "Watch out," she whispers in my ear, using her long shiny black hair to shield me from the girls' view. "The witch is on her broom."

"'Bout time, Dul-say." Vikki's voice cuts through the freezing air like a chainsaw. I fight the urge to climb back on the cart and zoom off. Her thick, dark hair conceals her face, but I don't need to read her expression. She's my biggest threat—she wants to be the star of the show and is just waiting for an opportunity to see me fail. Vikki isn't only a witch in the show . . . her real-life version starts with a "b", not a "w."

Even tiny Asha starts nagging me. "Our toes have grown icicles from the fog because you took your sweet time. Don't worry; I kept Sebastian warm in your absence." Her pink rouge glows in the moonlight against her skin. She plucks at Vikki's lace collar, but Asha's right-hand girl must be too iced to do more than move her eyes my way. "I told you that the *Teen Glam* picture would give her a big head."

Marcilla's piercing violet eyes, enhanced by contacts, penetrate me. "Well, at least the picture shaved down her big nose." Her sharp accent makes her words sting even more.

Asha and Vikki cackle. I want to tell them off, but our director walks over before I can open my mouth. I take a deep breath. Not getting renewed would almost be a relief. At least then, I would no longer have to take their abuse. But I also wouldn't be able to pay for college. Or the mortgage. Only a few more years, I tell myself.

Mr. Hallward ignores Marcilla. "Now that our high priestess has decided to grace us with her presence, we can begin. In today's scene, the coven is going to cast a spell for everlasting youth. Ria's mom has been cursed and will die when her eldest daughter turns fifteen."

Figures. My character, Ria—The Water Witch, is totally doomed. No doubt Mr. Mulberg is already writing her funeral scene so that it coincides with her *Quinceañera*.

"Witches, take your places on the five points of the pentacle." Mr. Hallward raises his voice like he's the Wizard of Oz himself.

We all climb to our risers and then wait as the trainers place our familiars next to us. The production guys pull me to my spot in the circle. The video editors will go back later and edit it to make me look like I'm flying. I look up at the full moon. Perfect night for this shot. The perfume of the bay laurel, ferns, firs, and sage makes me giddy.

The Coven is all about its abracadabra scenes. Mr. Hallward goes all out—with wind machines, spooky sounds, incandescent lights, and faux mist. Sometimes it takes us four hours to shoot one incantation. But luckily, we already rehearsed this scene a bunch of time during the week. The other witches and I stand on our own points, made from rocks, with a bonfire burning in the center. Marigolds have been placed in a ring around the rocks, and the ground glows with candlelight. Various tools and offerings line the surface of the altar that is in front of me: candles, incense, salt, herbs, rocks, fruit, pictures, a chalice, and my athamé, a ceremonial dagger.

Mr. Hallward signals. "And roll 'em."

Showtime. I walk around the girls, casting the circle with my athamé, careful not to cut myself with its two-inch blade.

"I cast the circle round and round, from earth to sky, from sky to ground.

I conjure now this sacred place, outside time and outside space.

The circle is cast; we are between the worlds."

My skin prickles with intensity. Though I've said these words before, this time their consonants seem crisper, more intense. Spikes of electricity ripple through my body as I become Ria.

Asha a.k.a. Esen—The Air Witch, begins the call to quarters. Holding her raven above her head, she releases him into the moonlight. Normally, the raven immediately returns to a perch held by his trainer, but tonight he enjoys his few minutes of freedom, circling the set before crashing into a sound machine. Asha ignores the commotion; she lights incense and places it on the altar. The strong musky scent fills the air.

"We summon the spirit of air.

I call the watchtower of the east.

Help us to keep our minds clear and open, and aid us in seeking positive change.

Come now and guard our circle."

Her voice sounds breathier than usual. Chills tingle through my spine as the special effects men blast us with wind.

Halia, Pele—The Fire Witch, places her iguana near the bonfire and throws a packet of sage into the flames. Where are the animal rights activists when we need them? Normally, we keep our familiars away from the fire. Poor little iguana could burn her toes!

"We summon the spirit of fire.

I call the watchtower of the south.

Element of passion and transformation, help us to make the choices that will lead to greater success in the months ahead.

Come now and guard our circle."

Halia's skin glistens, and her pupils dilate until she looks almost possessed. The bonfire blazes and singes the bottom of her cloak, but she doesn't even flinch, and our usually safety-conscious director doesn't cut the scene.

I pour water on the ground around Winter. The little guy's head pops up, and he hops away.

"We summon the spirit of water.

I call the watchtower of the west.

Open our hearts to love, our bodies to healing and our minds to wisdom from within and without.

Come now and guard our circle."

Water dances around the fire, dampening the flame.

Marcilla, Demi—The Earth Witch, scatters salt on her chinchilla, who seems to enjoy it and rolls on her back.

"We summon the spirit of Earth.

I call the watchtower of the north.

Nourish and ground us; help us connect to all the hidden strengths within ourselves.

Come now and guard our circle."

The salt seems to vanish before my eyes as if the hungry earth below our feet devoured it.

Vikki, Blythe—The Spirit Witch, lights a white taper and hoists her prairie dog toward the sky.

"Great Goddess, Lady of the Shining Moon and Shifting Tides, we, your daughters, gather here and invoke your name.

On this night of power and beauty, we come together in this sacred space and practice our craft.

Shine your light upon our circle, and lend us your strength and grace. Welcome, and blessed be."

We clasp our hands together, and the special effects team blazes a path of fire in between us—forming a pentagram of flames. I'm no longer acting—I feel the Goddess inside me. Her warmth and power fill my soul. My skin tightens, my breath quickens. Normally, I think of these scenes as nothing more than a job, but this night, for the first time, I believe that I'm creating real magic. My vision blurs, and the image of a handsome boy, with perfect skin, haunted eyes, and plump lips, flashes before my eyes. The ground under my body rumbles, and I begin to vigorously tremble causing me to bite my lip so hard that I taste my own tart blood in my mouth.

We've filmed spell scenes more times than I can count, and I've never had a reaction like this. My eyes dart everywhere and land on Mr. Hallward. He gives me two big thumbs up and sports a wide smile like he's pleased with the scene.

Except, it isn't right.

Something's taking over me. I sneak a couple of deep breaths.

I open my faux *The Book of Shadows* and place it on the altar. Before I speak, I pause and stare at my *Teen Glam* cover stuffed in the book.

A wicked thought passes through my head.

This photo will never age, but I will grow old and wrinkly. I wish I could stay young forever and that picture could age. That would be the coolest thing ever! I would do anything for that. To look like that forever, I would sell my soul.

No sooner than the idea formulates in my head do the lights above me flicker on and off. A rush of adrenaline surges through my body, and shimmery zig-zag lines flash in front of my eyes like I'm about to get a migraine.

Then a chill passes over me as I remember the plot of my favorite book, *The Picture of Dorian Gray*. Dorian made the same wish to his painter and was doomed to remain young while his picture aged.

But that could never happen in real life . . . could it?

I signal the start of the spell, setting the rest of the girls in motion.

Vikki lights one black candle. With my right hand, I take the chalice of water that Asha sets before me. Marcilla adds salt and two spoonsful of the herb vervain to the water. She mixes it thoroughly, dips a piece of petrified wood into the chalice, and then takes the chalice from my hand and gives me a rock. I pass the rock through the flame of the candle and chant:

"Candle, herb, rock, water, salt.

Hear me as my song is sung,

Age is not my heart's desire.

It is youth to which I aspire.

Candle, herb, rock, water, salt."

I touch the rock in turn to one foot, one hand, one shoulder, the crown of my head, and then down the other side of my body to shoulder, hand, and foot. Each time I repeat the chant, my fingers tingle. My legs quiver as I throw the rock in a nearby stream with a shaking hand. Maybe I'm ill. I'm usually calm and mellow when I film. I try to wiggle my frozen toes. Asha's right—the San Francisco fog is chilling.

After a moment of silence, we join hands. A chilling stream of mist sprinkles on our bodies. A cosmic shock travels through our circle. The girls and I let out a collective scream. The shock isn't in the script, but I can't seem to turn my head to see if the special effects team are scrambling to correct whatever they just messed up. Electrocuting a group of teenagers won't look good on their resumes.

Images pass in front of my eyes like I'm stuck in a video game: Vikki sprinkling powder over a dead boy, Halia vanishing into thin air, Marcilla hovering over a gorgeous girl, and Asha walking through a ring of fire. The images blind me, coming so hard and so fast that my knees wobble and it takes everything I have to stay on my feet.

Thankfully, the whir of the mist machines cuts through the fog in my brain, and a soft blanket of tiny water droplets starts to fall around us.

"And cut!" Mr. Hallward punches the air in victory as reality slams me. I'm just Dulce again, and my coven has reverted into a bunch of backstabbing wannabe megastars.

"Girls, that was great," Mr. Hallward says. "Dulce, you were excellent today. You nailed that spell. Great touch biting your lip and letting the blood drip down your face." He throws his arms around me in a big bear hug.

I cringe and let my hands dangle at my sides. Mr. Hallward isn't one to randomly hug.

"You look somehow different as if you're almost glowing." He lets me go and then rushes off to check the video playback.

Halia comes over and takes my hand. "Duls, you okay? Your hand was shaking all crazy when I held it during the scene."

I can barely make out her face, but her tanned skin looks shiny in the moonlight. "Yeah, sorry. I'm like dizzy. Was it just me or did something spooky just happen?"

"Well, the scene was pretty intense, but it wasn't spooky." She laughs as she eyes me up and down skeptically. "You drink too many iced mochas. Mark my words, those things are gonna kill you."

I roll my eyes. "I know, but they taste so good! I'm addicted."

She stares at me. "Whoa, girl! Your eyes look crazy gold—like you are possessed! Are you wearing those colored contacts again?"

"Seriously? You know I told costuming that I would never put those on again. They burned my pupils. I couldn't see for a week."

She tilts her head to get a closer look, but I pull away and close my eyelids. "It's probably just the lighting." As I open my eyes, she blows me a kiss and then hops on her own golf cart. "Tomorrow, you and me, dinner before the scene? I have to tell you about Asha and the key grip. Mr. Hallward found them kissing and—" She clamps her hand over her mouth, and her eyes shift. "I'll tell you all about it tomorrow." She gives me a "call me" hand sign.

I flash her the sign back.

The rest of the girls disperse without saying goodbye, which is not surprising. I scoop up Winter in his crate, my faux *The Book of Shadows,* and then climb back into the cart, shielding my face with my hand.

It's always so weird being back in my trailer right after a scene this late at night. There aren't any people shouting reminders through the door, my makeup artist isn't trying to get me to sit still, there aren't crew members working outside. It's all so . . . quiet. Sometimes it's hard to know if I've truly left the make-believe world and entered the real one.

I'm too tired to really contemplate it. I just want to hurry up and get out of this costume so I can go home and crash. I release Winter from his crate, and I exhale a deep sigh as I grab some cleansing towelettes from the counter and scrub off my makeup while looking at the huge mirror on the wall. I can't see that smile line around my mouth. Huh, maybe the hemorrhoid cream Mr. Mulberg gave me to put on my face really did work.

I stare at myself closer, my attention wholly on the tiny gold flecks in my eyes. And my lips are perfectly plump. "That's weird..."

I shove my face right up to the mirror. My nose looks smaller than usual. I rub my finger over the bridge and can't even feel a hint of a bump. And the big zit I had on my forehead earlier has vanished. Okay, this is totally bizarre. I must be more tired than I think.

Then the craziest thought pops into my head: *What if that youth spell really worked?*

No, that's stupid. I don't believe in all that magic as my Nana did. Things like that don't happen in real life.

Or do they?

I flip open *The Book of Shadows* and look at the *Teen Glam* cover again. The flecks in the snapshot have disappeared, and there are faint wrinkles around my mouth, my nose is so not airbrushed— and smack in the middle of my forehead is a huge zit.

I slam the book shut and stuff it in my purse for safe keeping.

"Ay!" What is going on? The room seems to be spinning. I must be hallucinating; it's the only explanation. The caffeine probably made me jittery.

Breathe, Dulce. Breeeeathe.

I look back in the mirror and do a mental checklist. Skin—translucent and glowing. Hair—straight and frizz-free. Nose—cute as a button. These flecks really brighten my face. Flecks the color of my 14-carat-gold key necklace.

I have to force myself to breathe, and my chest heaves from the effort.

Then I grab my Talavera vase and hurl it at the mirror, shattering the glass. Shards jump at my face. I duck, but it's useless—the sharp slice tears into my forehead before my hands are even raised. Warm blood trickles down my cheeks, and I collapse to my knees, hitting my head before it touches the floor.

And then I see him.

The most beautiful boy, standing above me—round crimson lips, penetrating violet eyes, ivory skin, and shiny golden hair.

The room becomes blurry, and the last thing I remember is Winter cuddling next to my chest, cooing contently.

THE TALK

*It is silly of you, for there is only one thing in the world worse than being **talked** about, and that is not being talked about.*

— OSCAR WILDE, THE PICTURE OF DORIAN GRAY

CHAPTER 3

I wake hoping to catch a glimpse of the intoxicating boy from my vision. Instead, I hear the irritating voice of an entertainment reporter on television.

"We are live outside Marin General Hospital, where *The Coven* star Dulce Garcia was rushed last week. Though her PR team has yet to issue a statement, inside sources tell us that sixteen-year-old Dulce collapsed two weeks ago after suffering complications from extensive plastic surgery and has been in a medically induced coma ever since."

Two weeks? I've been in a coma? I try to speak but am unable to produce any sound. Both my agent, Rosa, and my auntie, Maria, have their backs turned to me, their faces glued to the television.

The reporter continues with her lies. "A source on the set of *The Coven* said that Dulce was late for filming that day and that while he didn't see her before the shoot, after filming her face looked very smooth and tight, and her eyes were incandescent."

I've had enough. I wiggle my body and try to shake the hospital bed, but no one notices. I finally clap my hands loudly.

Luckily, the clamor alerts Maria. "Dulce, *mija*, you're awake! We were so worried! How are you feeling?" She comes to my side and puts her hand on my face. As Maria hugs me, I hear the reporter asking an expert plastic surgeon for an opinion on the effects of Botox on a sixteen-year-old. Rosa turns the television off.

I ignore Maria's question. "Why am I hooked up to an IV? I was in a coma?"

Maria sits next to me and strokes my hair. "The doctor did it, Dulce. They put you in a coma because your brain showed swelling. And yes, you've been in a coma since the night of the shoot."

"Ouch! You're pulling my hair!" I screech.

The next shriek, however, isn't mine.

Maria cups my face in her hands. "Dulce. What did you do to yourself? You're gorgeous!"

I push her hands off me. "Thanks, Tía Maria. Was I hideous before?"

"Of course, she didn't mean that." Rosa gives me her signature evil grin—the one I only see when she's just signed a new endorsement or sold my soul to the Savvy executives. "It's just that you look so much better, even though you could still fix your weak chin. Don't get me wrong—I'm happy you made the *responsible* choice to get a touch-up—I just wish you'd consulted us first."

"I didn't get 'a touch up'! I don't even know what happened. All I know is after the night shoot we said this spell . . ."

Maria interrupts, "Really, Dulce. Don't start talking all crazy on us." She ignores me and turns to Rosa. "What are we going to do?"

"Don't panic, Maria. We can spin this, too." Rosa bites her nails. "We can say that Dulce tried a new facial with crushed diamonds. This could be a wonderful opportunity. She could endorse a new acne line for teens. Her skin is completely clear now. And maybe she could sell lip kits to explain her new plumpness." She pinches my cheeks, which are inexplicably throbbing. "How could you go get Botox and a nose job without telling anyone? What's the name of the doctor? I should see to it that he loses his medical license for treating a minor even though you are emancipated. But it would get into the tabloids, so I won't." She gets a hard look on her face, the one I've learned to stay far away from. "Who took you? It was Eva, right? I never liked her."

I can't believe this. My own team is buying the gossip? "Are you serious? I didn't get any injections—I swear. It was, well, I don't know, it had to have been the spell."

"The spell?" Maria asks.

"Yeah, the spell. See, the coven was doing a spell for everlasting youth. It must've worked." They're inching closer together as if to protect themselves from the crazy explanation I'm giving them. I decide to change course. "Never mind, I don't believe it myself. Maybe it was that new face cream Eva bought me."

A nurse barges in the door, and we all fall silent. She leans over the foot of my bed like she's going to check my chart—only she has an iPhone tucked in her palm and snaps a picture of me like she's all sly and we don't all just see that.

"Hey!" Maria knocks the phone out of the nurse's hand, snatches it up from the ground, and plunks it into a cup of water on my nightstand.

Rosa corners the woman. "Sorry, missy," Rosa slaps her hands together like she's dusting off dirt, "we already have an exclusive photo shoot scheduled with *YES* magazine on Friday. If you pull anything like this again, I'll call the cops." She stirs the phone around with her finger.

At that, Rosa opens the door and points. The nurse slinks out of the room. "Honestly," Maria closes the door and locks it, "people would sell their mothers for a few bucks. Where's the integrity in this world? Where's the compassion? Everyone thinks some little girl's been mutilated, and all they see are dollar signs." She freezes, and her eyes cut to me. "Oh, Dulce, hon, I'm sorry—"

"A mirror," I say flatly. Remembering the way the glass had shattered and the searing pain across my face.

"*Mija*," Maria reaches for my hand. "It's not what you think."

"I need a mirror!" I cry.

Maria nods slowly at Rosa, who obediently gives me her compact.

I hold it up to my face. Supposedly, I've been in a coma for two weeks, but I would never have known it. I look amazing. My hair is shiny, my nose is sleek, my eyes are bright, my lips are pouty, and my skin is radiant. My forehead is clear as the San Francisco Bay on a fogless day. I expected to have a red dot between my eyes like an Indian princess. "Where's the cut from the other night? A huge piece of glass impaled my forehead, I felt it. See! I told you it was the spell. How else do you all explain that there's no mark?"

Maria stares at me. "I saw glass next to your head, but I don't think that it actually hit you."

This is ridiculous. "Tía, it did to hit me!"

She shakes her head and looks at me with critical eyes. "You should've told me, *mija*. Maybe I would've let you do it. Maybe I would've done it *with* you. I am your family. I need to know everything." Her lips pucker, and I can see the lines on her mouth. I knew it—she's just jealous because she thinks that I didn't take her to get fillers with me.

"This is crazy." I shove the flimsy hospital blanket off my lap and sit up. A bit of head-rush hits me, but with the room as cold as it is, I refocus pretty quickly. "After everything we've been through, you're going to believe tabloid rumors over me? I swear if either of you says another word about me having plastic surgery, I'll quit. I will. I don't care about this stupid show or even being an actress or how much money I'll have to pay to break my contract. I told you I didn't get any work done. If you don't believe me, that's your problem. But I won't sit here and listen to it!"

Rosa's reaction is typical. Pinched lips and another skeptical look. I want to tell her to stop making a face because it will give her wrinkles, but I'm so upset I don't care. "Dulce, let's just agree to disagree." Rosa never dares to speak against me, even if she thinks I'm lying. She's too afraid to upset me because I'm her highest profile client. "Let's just move forward and get ready for your magazine shoot."

She tries to give me a hug, but I turn away. "Forget the shoot. I'm not going to do it. Rosa, release any statement you want. I don't care. Both of you. Leave!"

Without another word, I turn over in my narrow hospital bed and proceed to completely ignore them, which isn't hard. It takes them a whole minute to walk out of the door. When the soft click sounds, I exhale deeply and close my eyes, thinking about the events that brought me here. I just keep circling back to the guy I saw right before I passed out. It must have been a hallucination. He was beautiful, and I don't think I had ever seen anyone who looked so flawless. Maybe I saw his picture somewhere, but where? He was classically handsome. Like he belonged in an art gallery. Or the Louvre.

Three steady knocks sound, and I groan. "Tía! I want to be left alone!"

"Sorry to disturb you," a husky voice with a crisp British accent says.

"I'm not your mum, but I was wondering if I could speak with you for a moment."

Where's my security team? Must be a reporter from *CHAT* magazine. Who knew the Brits were interested in my story? "Not now. You can make up your trash without a quote from me."

The door opens anyway, but I stay facing away from the door. If this guy is here for a picture, he's only getting one of the back of my head. I'm reaching for the call button on the bed rail when he speaks again, stopping my hand.

"Miss Garcia, I presume. I'm humbled to make your acquaintance. I'm Dorian Gray."

What the —? "Wow, your parents must've been literature majors. Pretty arrogant name choice." I take the risk of peeking over my shoulder at the boy—not man—smiling at me. His smile brightens, although there's something slightly sinister and a bit crooked about it.

I take in his features, stunned.

He is the boy from my vision.

THE TRUTH

*It is perfectly monstrous the way people go about nowadays saying things against one behind one's back that are absolutely and entirely **true**.*

— OSCAR WILDE, THE PICTURE OF DORIAN GRAY

CHAPTER 4

I snap out of it. I'm being completely ridiculous. I was hallucinating that night. I'm probably hallucinating now!

He can't be more than eighteen. His eyes are the color of my amethyst ring, and his lips look like plump *pan dulce*. Dressed in a polo shirt, khaki shorts, and loafers, he gives off an East Coast prep school vibe.

He chuckles. "No, actually they weren't. The notoriety came after Mr. Wilde wrote about me."

Does this guy seriously want me to believe he's the famous gothic character? I reach into my purse and text Halia.

Dulce: Come get me now!

"Don't come any closer or I'll scream! Who are you? Dorian Gray isn't real; he's a fictional character. And even if he ever existed, he's dead. Maybe *you* haven't read the book." He does look too perfect to be real, but that's beside the point. His features are as if an artist drew them.

I glance at my phone, grateful that my bestie has already responded.

Halia: On my way!

"I'm very real. *The Picture of Dorian Gray* was a biography of sorts. I paid Oscar Wilde a handsome sum to tell my story. He did take some liberties with the truth . . ." He regards the phone in the glass of water for a moment. "I can assure you, Miss Garcia, I'm not dead. Wilde killed me off in the book because it made for a better ending. Something about giving the story a moral. "Virtue wins over vanity," he said. I've been alive and haven't aged for over one hundred years. I can't explain it. Like a vampire, except I don't have to drink blood."

This is ridiculous. I'm a rational, intelligent teenager. I don't believe in immortal beings.

But then again, until that night shoot, I hadn't believed in spells either. "I get it. This is some stupid reality prank show, isn't it? Where are the cameras?"

His eyes twinkle. "No, I don't watch much television. I find it mindless. I prefer live theater. Though, I have watched one of your episodes. You, my dear, are a brilliant actress. You remind me of a girl who once had my heart."

Is this guy serious? "Sibyl Vane, I presume?"

He doesn't dignify my question with a response, and a pained look graces his face.

"Fine, *Mr. Gray*. I'll play. What are you doing in Marin?"

He comes closer to me. Too close. I want to pull away, but he smells yummy—like fresh cut pine and shaved cinnamon. I'm rendered helpless. "I believe you've succumbed to my curse."

Now he's scaring me. I grind my teeth. "My curse? How do you know what happened to me? The tabloids don't even have the story straight."

"I can't explain it, really. I woke up one night and knew another

44

person had uttered a mad wish. Ever since I read about what happened to you, I felt a pull. And one look at you, and I know I'm right."

This guy is probably some seriously unstable stalker. Just to be safe, I clutch the emergency hospital call button but hold off on pressing it. "You're insane. You were cursed when you wished out loud to remain young and have your picture age. I did nothing of the sort," I lied.

I did make the same wish. But it was a silent wish. While I was doing the spell. No one heard me.

"Allow me to prove it." He walks over and yanks the IV out of my arm.

"What are you doing?" I jerk back, totally expecting blood to gush out, but no. Not a drop of blood. The IV comes out smooth as my abuela's caramel flan.

I examine my arm closely. The puncture mark vanishes before my eyes.

His cold hand touches my cheek. "You know I'm telling the truth."

I flinch back. "I know nothing of the sort. Please leave immediately. I just need some time. Time to figure out what happened. There *must* be a logical explanation for this."

He laughs. "I'll give you all the time you need. After all, we have eternity." He pauses and studies me. "Where's your picture?"

How does he know about the picture? "I don't know what you're talking about."

He nods his head. "Sure, you don't. Dulce, find your picture and never let it out of your sight."

"Don't tell me what to do," I snap. But I can feel anxiety creep up in my chest. Is he serious? Have I really turned into my picture? Where is that stupid book anyway? Finally, I remember, I put it in my purse. I spy my purse in the corner, but I don't dare get out of bed to grab it while Dorian is here.

Dorian reaches into his pocket and strums his car keys. "May I take you to lunch? I'd like to get to know you better."

Lunch with this guy doesn't sound like a good idea. I don't trust Dorian, or myself with him for that matter. I need backup.

"Well, in case you can't see. I'm currently in the hospital. I can't just up and bounce. I have to get discharged and stuff." But part of me doesn't want him to leave. Not only is he hot, but I'm also drawn to him. And there is a part of me that thinks that maybe he could be telling me the truth. "Maybe later today like at two? I'm sure I'll be out of here by then. My friend Halia is picking me up in a bit. There's this great café in Larkspur. It's just down the street— Emporio Rulli on Magnolia."

"That sounds delightful. I love downtown Larkspur. It's very quaint. Yes, see you then." He starts out the door but then stops and turns around. "Dulce, would you mind keeping our conversation about what has happened to you and my identity a secret? Just for now."

I never keep secrets from Halia; she's more like a sister to me than a friend.

But I know Dorian is right. "Fine, I won't tell her, but not because you asked me to keep it a secret. I just want to understand every-thing better myself." The last thing I want to do is have Halia babbling to everyone that I'm cursed. Because I'm not. Or maybe I am. I don't know.

I love her, but that girl always exaggerates. She's super dramatic.

Dorian gives me a smug smile. My shoulders tense.

"Perfect, Dulce. I'll see you tomorrow." And he walks out the door.

I slip into the bathroom and change out of my hideous hospital gown. I call the nurse to check myself out of the hospital. One of the benefits of being a teen actress is that I was able to be legally emancipated so I could work so many hours on the set, especially for night shoots. This freedom gives me the ability to make all legal decisions about my life. It's only fair. I figure since I financially support myself, I'm definitely mature enough to call all the shots in my personal life.

Then, I look in my bag to make sure I have the faux *The Book of Shadows*. It's right there. I pause and take a deep breath and examine the book.

I flip it over and rip the fake jacket off. It's just an anthology, right? An anthology of monsters and spells and zombies and magic. Oh no! I said my spell over all that? How could I be so stupid?

I open the anthology to where my picture is and study it. My zit is inflamed, my hair has flyaways galore, my schnoz looks huge, my thin lips are almost nonexistent, and my blotchy skin seems even ruddier. And right in the middle of my eyes is a huge red scar right where the mirror had cut me that night. And my arm in the picture has a bloody mark where my IV had been. I try to rub it off—maybe the lipstick in my purse somehow smudged it. But the harder I rub, the darker the mark on the picture becomes.

This couldn't be happening. Dorian couldn't be right. Could he?

I peel back the *Teen Glam* picture to figure out which stories I'd jammed it between—Edgar Allan Poe's *The Oval Portrait* and Oscar Wilde's *The Picture of Dorian Gray*.

Uh oh.

Yvonne once told me that *The Oval Portrait* was the basis for Wilde's book. *The Picture of Dorian Gray* is my favorite book. Dorian falls in love with his painting and wishes he could look like that forever. He stays young, and every time he does something bad, the picture ages. One day, he can't take it anymore, and he stabs the portrait and dies.

But Dorian is very much alive if that's really him.

No! Have I turned into my picture? Did I just make a pact with *El Diablo*? If someone destroys this photo, will I die as Dorian did? Am I going to stay sixteen forever? Savvy Network would love that—they'll never let me out of my contract!

¡Ay, Dios mío!

I slam the book shut and take some calming breaths. This is worse than I could ever imagine. Not a Wiccan spell, but a curse. I am cursed!

I'll never grow old. Never go to college. Never get married. Never have beautiful bilingual babies with Sebastian. Why had I wished for such a stupid thing? Teens want to be older, not younger.

But after a few minutes, I have a realization. Maybe, it isn't so bad. Maybe, it is a blessing.

Savvy will never fire me. I'll be able to support myself. I'll never need anyone.

For the first time in what seems like forever, I don't feel all tense and rushed.

And I like it.

Dorian was right. I already do know. I've had more than enough proof even before he walked in. I'm like him. I'm enchanted somehow. I will stay young forever.

Forever.

THE SECRET

*I have grown to love **secrecy**. It seems to be the one thing that can make modern life mysterious or marvelous to us. The commonest thing is delightful if only one hides it.*

— OSCAR WILDE, THE PICTURE OF DORIAN GRAY

CHAPTER 5

My heart races. I want to believe that this mysterious spell has just changed my life forever. But I need more proof. I need to speak to Dorian alone.

The door flies open again, and I see wisps of Halia's long black hair hanging over a huge sunflower arrangement.

"Oh my gosh, Duls. You okay? Girl, you look amazing!" She puts the flowers on the nightstand and embraces me. "And who's that totally hot guy I just bumped into in the hallway?" Her eyes dance. "I saw him leaving your room while I was signing in the at the visitor's desk."

"Close the door."

Halia flashes a huge smile, slams the door shut, and hops on the bed.

Who's Dorian exactly? "That's Dorian, um, he's just an old family friend." I pause because I know she'll be meeting him in a bit, so I want to make my story believable. "Our dads were friends forever ago. We knew each other as kids. He's about to transfer to Redwood."

A framed picture of a basket that adorned the bleak hospital wall crashes down to the ground, the glass flying everywhere. I flinch back and Halia shrieks.

"Whoa, that's dangerous. They probably hung that up with tape."

My chest throbs. Am I like a female Pinocchio now? Will I have a physical reaction to every lie I tell?

Halia picks the picture off the ground and brushes the glass aside with her shoe. "Well, I'm mad I haven't met him yet. He's smoking hot. Is he single?"

"Um, I'm not sure. I think so. He did mention something about an ex-girlfriend that he was totally in love with—Sibyl." I so want to tell her the whole crazy story, but I force myself to hold back. Not only because Dorian asked me to, but also because I want to be sure before I start telling everyone that I'm cursed.

"Sibyl and Dorian. Super ancient names. Well, I hope he has some gorgeous friends. I know you're hung up on Sebastian and all, but Dorian is way sexier."

"I'm not 'hung up' on Sebastian. We're just friends."

"Whatever. Anyway, what happened to you?" As if Halia can sense my hesitation, she pulls the edge of my dress and drops her voice to a whisper. "No one else is here. Tell me. Your skin, hair, and eyes look so great. I promise not to breathe a word to a soul."

I don't know what to say, so I spit out the excuse my agent is going to use. "I got a facial and a Brazilian blowout." I pause and focus my gaze on the ceiling lights, praying that they won't come crashing down on me.

She squints her eyes at me and doesn't look convinced.

I continue to fib. "Yeah, I mean look at the gold in my eyes. It's these new colored contacts."

"But you told me that you'd never wear those things again. I thought they burned your eyes."

I did tell her that. Some actress I am. "Yeah, but these are a new brand. They're lubricated. Way better."

She leans in close to me and touches my smooth face. "That's what I told everyone. There is no way we would ever get plastic surgery. Marci, Vik, and Ash maybe, but so not us." She pauses and then leans into me. "But you know what? Something super weird is going on." Her voice drops to a whisper tone. "That night after the spell, I was super sick. I went back to my trailer and puked everywhere. It was so gross. Then I had crazy dreams all night about being invisible! It was actually kind of cool. I could just slip in and out of parties, and no one even knew I was there. In the dream, I crashed this costume party or something, and there was this super-hot guy there. He was the only person who seemed to be able to see me . . . and then he completely disappeared too. He was like an invisible man."

I swallow hard, the wind nearly knocked out of me. Reaching for the pitcher of water to pour myself a glass, I knock the flower arrangement down and spill water all over the sheets. Had Halia transformed also? What about the other girls? I hadn't even read *The Invisible Man*. What's going to happen to her?

I start cleaning up the flowers and then finally pour myself a glass of water and down it. "Halia, listen to me. Did anything else weird happen to you that night? Have you seen the other girls lately?"

Halia places a rogue sunflower back into the vase. "Nothing else weird has happened. Though at school lately they all seem a little off, but they're always so self-absorbed. Marci was hitting on this new girl, Ash was flirting with not one but two boys, and I caught her smoking a clove on break. And now that you mention it . . ." she sucks in a breath and looks at me with wide eyes. "Oh my God, Vik had a complete meltdown in pre-chemistry, she was acting like a total psycho. We were dissecting frogs and she was trying to bring one back to life! Do you believe that?"

Yes, because I may have bewitched all four of you. I reach into my bag and pull out my anthology. Scanning the index, I see that it includes H. G. Wells' *The Invisible Man.*

Fabulous. Everything is starting to make sense to me now. I've given my costars gothic superpowers. What will happen to Asha, Marcilla, and Vikki?

"Listen to me. I need you to tell me if anything, even if it's a small thing, strange happens to you. I, um, I felt weird after the scene also."

Halia's brows lift, and she purses her lips. "Do you think we created real magic? Oh my gosh, Dulce—that would be so cool. Maybe we really are true witches."

"No, it wouldn't be cool. I'm not saying that at all. I just want to make sure we didn't get sick or anything from all the candles and herbs we always have to use."

I need to drop this subject before she starts connecting the dots. "Do you want to meet Dorian?" I'm sure of the answer to this question. Halia is always up for meeting boys. "You can ask him if he has any hot friends."

"Seriously? Do you even need to ask?" Halia grabs my flowers, and I gather the rest of my belongings. I shut the door of my hospital room and begin the process of checking out. It takes what seems like forever.

When I'm finally processed out, Halia and I sneak down the service elevator and exit through the back door to avoid the paparazzi. I can't avoid them forever. They will start asking even more questions once new pictures of me are released. But I can't stress about that. I need some answers from Dorian. He's the only one who might be able to help me.

I put on my oversized sunglasses and scan the parking lot for paparazzi. They're everywhere—totally baffling. We are in Marin, not Los Angeles. Did they all drive up after news broke about my face?

"Allow me." Halia tries to use my big floral arrangement as a shield from the paparazzi, but it's hopeless. I can already see the headlines. "Dulce Garcia Flees Hospital with Costar to Meet Mysterious Stranger." The flashes blind me as I slide into the Halia's Audi R8, the slick leather caressing my skin.

"So where to, Duls?"

"Emporio Rulli." "Awesome. I'm craving a vanilla latte." She guns the engine, losing the paps in a complicated crisscross of different side streets and cut-throughs. She's good, too. I've lived here all of my life, and I didn't recognize three of the alleys she took. Then, when she's sure no one is following us, she cuts into the parking lot of the café.

Halia pulls into the last open spot, which is right under a flag that has a picture of a girl in a boat holding a parasol. It reads "Larkspur, 100 years."

I wonder what the town looked like back then. If Dorian is telling the truth, maybe he can tell me.

We exit the car and walk into the red brick building. I scan the room for Dorian, but I don't see him anywhere. Halia orders her vanilla latte and then wanders over to marvel at the pastries set in neat lines inside the case.

"Good café choice. Very European." His voice is soft and so close to my ear it sends a shiver of goose bumps down my spine. I turn just enough to see him from the corner of my eye, but his attention is turned to Halia. "And you must be the beautiful and talented Haliana Griffin. I'm a huge fan. My name is Dorian Gray." He grasps her hand and kisses it.

Halia completely falls for his charm. "Pleased to meet you, Mr. Gray. Do you have a red room of pain?"

I pinch her. Dorian smirks.

"Just teasing. Couldn't resist. Call me Halia. I'm so excited that you're moving here." She tosses her silky hair and flashes him a grand grin.

"I'm very excited as well. Let's order, shall we?"

Halia sits down at an orange marble table and takes out her iPhone.

He signals to the cute barista, "We'll have a large vanilla latte, a double espresso, a plate of the gnocchi, a Milanese Panini, a torta, and an almond brioche."Whoa, carbs. "Um, thanks, Dorian, but I'll have a non-fat organic sugar-free vanilla latte and the red endive salad, dressing on the side."

He squeezes my hand, but his fingers are cold and clammy. "You still don't get it," he whispers. "You can eat whatever you want now and not gain an ounce or get those unsightly pocks on your face."

Pocks? He must mean acne. Luckily, I've read enough literature from his time period to have a clue what he's talking about. I also took Latin as a freshman and am now studying for the SAT, so I have a good handle on his vocabulary. "Um okay, then I'll keep it as a real latte the way he ordered it. And can I get a cheese plate with brie?"

Dorian pays, and we join Halia at the small table. Typical Marinites surround us. Two gorgeous, super-fit mommies without a hint of makeup who have toddlers in running strollers sit to our left. A long-haired hippy dude in Birkenstocks is sipping green tea behind us. Two well-dressed men cuddle in the corner. No one acts like they recognize me, except maybe the barista. There are only a few celebrities in Marin. But luckily, no one seems to really care. And I love that.

Halia taps my toes under the table. "So, Dorian. Are you single?"

She certainly doesn't waste any time.

"Yes, in fact, I am. It's hard to find a girl who understands me." He gives me a longing glance, but I look down.

"Yeah. Same with me. Like most guys think it's cool that I'm on television, but I can never tell if they like me for me or if they just want to get famous. Dulce and I are both super single."

Way to be subtle, Halia. "Thanks. But unlike my dear costar, I'm not interested in dating." Another lie. The truth is I'm only interested in dating Sebastian.

Halia's phone beeps, and she looks at the screen. "Lame. I have to go home. My mom's acting crazy. You're so lucky you don't have a mom, Duls."

I wince but cover it. "Yeah. No one can tell me what to do."

Halia doesn't even pick up on how her words hurt me. "Dorian, can you give Dulce a ride home?"

Is she serious? Ditching me with some stranger? I would never do that to her. But I can take care of myself. "That won't be necessary Dorian. I have a ride." I wink hard at Halia and text Sebastian to come get me. There's no way I'm getting into a car with Dorian.

"Okay. I'll catch you later. Nice to meet you, Dorian. Maybe we can hang out together some time and you can bring some friends." She flashes a huge smile and asks the barista to put her latte into a to go cup.

I excuse myself from Dorian's table and sneak up behind Halia. "So, what do you think of him?"

The barista hands Halia her latte. "Um, he's hot. Super hot. And he totally wants you. Go for it, Duls."

"I don't know." I can't tell her what Dorian said to me earlier, and honestly, it scares me.

Halia puts her hand on my shoulder. "Listen, Duls, you need to start living your life and having some fun. Ever since your dad died, you've acted all serious. All you ever do is study and work. Let your hair down, live a little. It's been years, and Sebastian has never asked you out. I'm not trying to hurt your feelings but you need to move on. Just give Dorian a chance."

Of course I've been serious ever since my dad died. I'll never forget the day that two Marines wearing Dress Blues knocked on my door and destroyed my world. I'd always been daddy's little girl. Now, I had no one.

But even so, her words cause me to wince. I'd be lying if I didn't admit to myself that I am still holding out hope for having a chance with Sebastian.

Then she blows a kiss toward me and leaves.

I make my way back to the table and sit next to Dorian.

"Well she seems lovely. I have a friend who would fancy her."

Who? The Invisible Man? I don't bother to ask.

He leans in closer to me. "So, tell me exactly what series of events took place that night?"

"I don't know. It was all so weird. I mean . . ." I hesitate, unsure of where I should start. I take a deep breath and decide to start from the beginning. "See, last month I did a photo shoot for *Teen Glam*. It was standard and all, so I didn't give it that much thought or anything. But then when I saw the picture on Instagram two weeks ago, and I was blown away."

His eyes twinkle with a hint of mischief, but he remains silent, so I keep going.

"Then, Winter, my bunny, ate *The Book of Shadows*—my prop for the show. So, I replaced it with this anthology of Victorian supernatural fiction. It's super cool—your story is in there. It's actually my favorite." Dorian smirks but still doesn't say a word. "So, I put *The Book of Shadows* cover on it and slipped my picture in between your book and Poe's *The Oval Portrait*. We said the spell of everlasting youth over the anthology. I felt all dizzy and stuff and then when I got back to my trailer, I looked like the picture." The barista brings our drinks, and I smile when I see the heart the barista has made in my foam. It's too pretty to drink.

Dorian takes a sip of his espresso. He seems so out of place here in this coffee house, in this town, in this time. I mean what teenager orders a double espresso?

"That's about it. I freaked out and threw a vase at the mirror. I must've passed out. Then I woke up in the hospital, and you showed up." I sip my latte, needing a second.

He squeezes his eyes shut and grits his teeth. As if he's worried about me. Or remembering his life. I've been doubtful about his claim, but something about the expression on his face makes me believe him.

"So, I'm seriously going to look like this forever? That's awesome. I have a photo shoot scheduled next week. I'll be the new *it* girl."

"No, it's not awesome. Dulce, you must not tell a soul about what happened. No one will understand anyway, and the public will think you are just one of those child starlets who had a mental breakdown. Your family could get you committed to a hospital under a crazy hold. Admit to cosmetic surgery or blame it on a necessary medical procedure for a deviated septum as all you celebrities seem to do. But under no circumstances should you tell anyone that you think something magical happened." He pauses and then offers, "And do the photo shoot."

Whoa buddy. I just met him and he's already telling me what to do. Controlling much? "I haven't decided about that yet. I'm not your Sibyl." I know all about his first love. I've read his story enough times. Dorian is beautiful and gallant and all, but what happened with her, with Sibyl . . . uh-uh, I'm not that pathetic. "I'm not going to poison myself if you don't like what I do."

He clenches his fist. "Please don't mention Sibyl. I find it upsetting." The tone of his voice is aching with regret. "She was very dear to me. And I was so young and still learning to live with my powers. Do what you must. I was just trying to say that, in my experience, it was easier to give the public what they want than try to hide."

The barista returns with the food—a big plate of gnocchi, roasted butternut squash, green pea puree, porcini mushrooms and a heaping scoop of Parmesan. I take a huge bite and the little pillows of pasta melt in my mouth. I don't remember food ever tasting this good; my taste buds seem sharper and all my senses are heightened. Maybe it's also the fact that this is the first meal since I've been cast on the show that I don't feel a twang of guilt indulging in since I know I can stuff my face and not gain an ounce. Well that, and I've been in a coma for two weeks.

"So, Dorian, how old are—I mean, were you?" "I was seventeen when I was painted, but that was one hundred and thirty years ago. But I'm still young at heart." And gorgeous. His eyes look almost amethyst and his lips are upturned. He could easily be a movie star or a model. Just wait until the Savvy executives see him. "So, Dulce, what's going on with you and Sebastian Vasquez?"

My insides chill. How does he know so much about me? "Why do you think anything is going on with him?"

"I read the periodicals."

"I don't see how it's any of your business." I consider following Eva's advice about maintaining mystery. But Dorian doesn't seem to be the kind of guy who plays games. "We're super close. We grew up together doing auditions, and he plays my boyfriend on my show. But we're *just* friends. He keeps me real." I watch Dorian's face to see if he can read my lie. Because the truth is, I'm in love with Sebastian. I always have been. I can't believe that I haven't told Sebastian about what happened to me yet.

Dorian reaches for my hand across the table. "Dulce, please, you must not tell Sebastian about your secret. He won't understand. In fact, it would be best if you kept some distance between you two, until you get a better handle on the consequences." That's it. I've had enough, even if Dorian is a gorgeous character from my favorite book of all time. I've done plenty of public service announcements about abusive relationships, and this guy is already demonstrating some troubling signs. "Look I really appreciate you flying all the way from England or wherever to 'help' me with my situation, but I think I have it under control. You already told me I'm not going to die, so I'm good. But you aren't going to tell me who I can hang out with. Especially since I've known Sebastian for like ever, and I met you like an hour ago." I stand up, leave a tip on the table. "So, it's been a pleasure meeting you." I feel an icy hand on my shoulder. "Dulce, I'm sorry, I didn't mean to upset you. I'm not trying to tell you what to do, but you need me. And times are different now. You are in the public eye. You can't just disappear like I did."

"I'll be fine."

He moves his hand from my shoulder to my wrist. "I made horrible mistakes because I didn't know how to live with my curse. People died, Dulce." His eyes are suddenly dark. "Two of them. This isn't some game. It's not about secrets. Don't make that mistake. Don't ever make that mistake."

His grip on my wrist is painful.

"You're hurting me," I whisper.

His eyes jump to his hand. He seems to relax and then let go. "This is serious. You need me. And I need you." I turn to him and can't help being drawn into his gaze. "Let me drive you home and just think about it."

Maybe I'm overreacting. Everything since the spell on the mountain has been a blur, and I'm not thinking clearly. Plus, I could learn so much about him and his life back in the Victorian Era. And he could help me write the best paper ever about *The Picture of Dorian Gray*. I have an AP Literature paper due this month.

"Sebastian will pick me up. I texted him when Halia left."

Dorian gives a heavy sigh. "I'll be staying at the Tiburon Lodge if you want to see me. I'm sorry I bothered you."

Great, now I don't know what to say. I fight a desire to reach out and hug him. Instead, I take a pen out of my bag and scribble down my cell phone number. "I need to rest, but we can talk tomorrow. Maybe we can meet up?"

Dorian's eyes glow. "I'd love to."His hand grazes my thigh. My skin tingles from his touch, but then I realize that my phone is vibrating, not his hand.

Sebastian: On my way! Saw the news. R u ok?"Bye, Dorian."

He leans in and kisses my hand. When his lips touch my skin, I see flashes of bright lights, massive pyramids, and ancient ruins. I close my eyes, and when I open them, Dorian has vanished.

I step outside and sit on a bench in front of the coffee house. Time, time. I need time. I'll figure this out.

I scan the road for Sebastian. After ten minutes, he pulls up on Magnolia Avenue.

"Hey, babe. I actually just left the hospital. I was trying to find you. Hop in."

I climb into his truck and place my hand on his knee. He gives me a cool kiss on the cheek. "Everything okay?"

"It is now that you're here."

He stares at my face, and I can almost see the millions of questions he has formulating in his head. "Do you want to tell me what happened?"

Sebastian has a way of making everything better for me without saying a single word. But even so, I decide to honor Dorian's wish and not immediately confess my secret to Sebastian.

I exhale. "I do. But not today. I'm overwhelmed."

He smiles and squeezes my hand. "It's okay. I'm here to talk when you're ready."

My frizz free hair floats in the wind as he drives me away from my favorite town.

THE PRICE

*Nowadays people know the **price** of everything and the value of nothing.*

— OSCAR WILDE, THE PICTURE OF DORIAN GRAY

CHAPTER 6

A few days later, my airbrushed face is on the cover of every tabloid in America. But this time the headlines aren't screaming, "Dulce—The Next Teen Idol." No. Overnight I've gone from beloved Savvy Network princess to the poster child for the perils of teen stardom.

I'm sprawled out on my Otomi embroidered bedspread, magazines strewn around me. "Dulce Garcia—Plastic Surgery at Sixteen?" is blazed over the cover of *Star* magazine.

"Did Savvy Network Pressure *The Coven* star to get Botox?" reads the headline of *US Weekly*.

My publicist did the best she could. She released a statement that I never had plastic surgery and that the changes to my appearance are the result of a powerful microdermabrasion facial, gold-flecked colored contacts, and a Brazilian keratin hair straightening treatment. The producers of the show have backed me up, stating that they could account for my whereabouts this month, which are chronicled by the paparazzi and my shooting schedule. But the media doesn't care about the fact that it was completely impossible for me to have had surgery before my accident.

"*Mija!*"

Maria pushes open my bedroom door without even knocking. She smells of lime and cumin—she's probably been cooking up a feast in anticipation of meeting Dorian since I invited him over for lunch. I told her Dorian was visiting his family and we'd met at Emporio Rulli. "Rosa's on the phone. The network wants to have a meeting about your contract."

That's a meeting I don't want to have. I'm sure they're going to fire me. "Tía, tell Rosa I'll call her later. I have to get ready for Dorian."

She points a wooden spoon at me. "Fine. But don't you forget you have the shoot coming up! Ever since you were released from the hospital, you've been acting flighty."

I ignore her and look down at my phone.

I want to flake on the photo shoot, but the network insists that I do it. Rosa has even arranged for a teen skin care line to sponsor the silly thing. She also somehow managed to get them to include the rest of the girls and Sebastian. I'm going to show up, I swear, but I'm just so nervous and want to make sure that this change is permanent first. What if while we are shooting my skin breaks out, and my nose grows back?

Not to mention, I still haven't worked up the courage to tell Sebastian what happened to me. What if he thinks I'm some deranged freak and he decides he wants nothing to do with me. I can't handle the thought of him rejecting me, so I've kept my mouth shut.

This is why I need to see Dorian today.

Apparently, Maria is still standing at my bedroom door. "*Pero, Rosa dice . . .*"

"I said later!" I slam the door. I can't shake the feeling that everyone is laughing at me because of all the tabloid stories. I still don't understand why so many people believe all that garbage.

I thumb through the *Life & Style* magazine, and I finally see one headline that really upsets me.

"Dulce Garcia Caught Cheating on Boyfriend Sebastian Vasquez!"

And there it is. A picture of Dorian and me at Emporio Rulli, snapped right as I was stuffing my face with gnocchi.

The caption reads, "Dulce left the hospital with a mysterious coed who was driving a flashy Lotus. Though his identity is still unknown, Dulce's representation has confirmed that he is simply an old family friend."

Nice cover, Rosa! Kind of funny that they think Dorian is a college coed—he does look super mature for seventeen, give or take about a hundred years. He totally has the east coast preppy university vibe going on. Like he's an attacker on lacrosse or captain of the crew team.

And Sebastian and I aren't even dating at all. Not to mention, I'd only met Dorian like ten minutes before the picture was taken. And we didn't leave the hospital together. Halia had given me a ride in her Audi. I would never get into a car with a strange guy. Why can they never get their stories straight?

I hate paparazzi. A girl can't even have a latte without being followed. I guess it could have been worse. We could have been in Coffee Bean & Tea Leaf in Beverly Hills. I don't even know how they found us.

Unless . . .

Could Dorian have tipped them off? Maybe he's selling info about me?

Tabloids are huge in the U.K. He could even be an undercover reporter? That would explain his accent and how he knew that I was at the hospital.

No, that's ridiculous—but it does make more sense than "I'm your favorite beloved immortal gothic literary character."

And my dumb ass believes him.

But as much as I tried to deny it, I keep coming back to the facts. My picture has changed, and my face looks like the picture before I said the spell. The IV Dorian pulled out of my arm didn't leave a mark.

I believe Dorian.

I don't have time to stress about the picture of us because Dorian is on his way to my house. I haven't really talked to him in the last couple of days. We've texted a few times, and he told me he was enjoying his time in the Bay Area. He'd already hit Alcatraz, Lombard Street, and Fisherman's Wharf.

I stumble out of bed, scrunch my feet into my fuzzy slippers, and hobble into the bathroom. Still not used to my curse, I stand in front of my mirror, expecting to see a mop full of frizzy flyaways and big brown circles under my eyes. Instead, staring back at me is the same gorgeous girl from the *Teen Glam* cover—shiny straight hair, glowing skin, and there are those dang flecks again.

I plug in my curling iron and wait for it to warm up, then thrust my face in a magnifying mirror and search for a zit. *Nada*—just flawless skin. I glow like the Noxzema girl.

"This curse is the best thing ever," I say aloud, even though there's no one to hear me, and reach for the curling iron.

"Ow!" I totally torch my finger. Sticking it in my mouth to suck on it, I want the throbbing to stop. And after a second or two, the pain's gone. I remove my finger from my mouth and watch as the burn mark fades away.

"What in the heck?" I get that I look like my picture, but scorching my flesh has no effect?

I take a deep breath and hold the scalding curling iron flush against my cheek.

"One Mississippi, two Mississippi . . ."

My skin feels almost icy before the pain begins. The smell of burnt flesh fills my nostrils, and there is such a searing heat against my cheek that my hand shakes. When black dots dance in front of my eyes, I drop the curling iron to the floor.

I grab the counter and grit my teeth, so I don't cry out and force my eyes to stay locked on the image in the mirror. A dark red line runs from my cheekbone to chin. For just the briefest second, I don't think it's going to go away, and panic twists in my stomach. I just held a red hot object to my face! My eyes prick with tears, and my breaths start to come in pants. Then, so very, very slowly the bright red fades from my skin.

¡Ay, Dios mío!

This is real. There are no doubts left now. Something had most definitely happened the night of the shoot. Am I possessed? Immortal? The only thing I know for certain is that burning one's skin with no reaction is not normal.

I resist the urge to scream for joy! My life will be easy now. I'll always look picture perfect. Which, in this day and age, is the key to success.

I try to smudge off my lipstick, but of course, it stays put. Thank God I like the makeup colors from the *Teen Glam* shoot because it seems like my face will look like this forever. I guess I'll be wearing

71

pink lipstick for the rest of the season. Savvy will probably have to digitally retouch my lips in winter to match our scarlet lipstick.

I pick up the iron again and try to twirl a tendril. After leaving it wrapped for the required thirty seconds, I release the clip. The curl cascades down into a little ringlet—and then straightens as if it has just been raked through a flat iron.

Then I try it again. And again. And again.

After the eighth attempt, I give up.

My chest feels light. From now on, I never will have to spend hours in makeup or hair. Think of all the time I can save. And I'll always look perfect for dates. I should've done this spell years ago!

But it can't all be this easy. I clench my teeth, worrying about my fate.

I brush my teeth and walk into my bedroom to get dressed. Scanning my closet, I slip on a pink satin slip dress. I feel like a princess, though the dress is a little loose. Running back to the bathroom, I step on the scale—one hundred and five pounds! I was one hundred and twenty pounds on the day of the *Teen Glam* photo shoot. I knew the editors airbrushed my picture. They aren't supposed to make teen starlets look too skinny, for the fear that young girls will become anorexic. Not a good thing—unlike my cast mates, I *hate* the way all the skinny Hollywood girls look. I like my body to be healthy and fit, and with my hipbones indenting both sides of this gown, I look sick. Sebastian is always saying how he hates super skinny girls and wants a girl with curves.

Well, at least my breasts are now big.

"Dulce! Dorian is here."

I slip into my rhinestone-encrusted sandals and head into the kitchen. Maria already has Dorian trapped by her tamales. My apricot-colored pug-chihuahua blend, Salsa, is nipping at his heels.

Maria swats Salsa with a rolled-up newspaper. "Salsa! I swear, Dulce, that *perrito sucio!*"

Salsa whimpers and turns her attention to my sandals.

"Dulce." Dorian stands and greets me. He looks even more handsome than he had a few days ago. Since I'd seen him last, I'd convinced myself that I only had eyes for Sebastian, but I swear my heart just skipped a beat. Wearing white knee-length shorts, a green and white Lacoste polo shirt and Vans, he must've gone shopping to fit in with the natives. "You look exquisite."

I try to mutter hello but instead squeak out a pathetic, "Hey."

Maria pours Dorian a huge glass of her signature watermelon *agua fresca.* "Dulce, Dorian just invited us to spend some time at his summer chateau in Nice. He says he owns a Matisse! I've always wanted to go to the South of France. *Oh là là.*"

I eye Dorian hard. Offering lavish gifts? Bragging? What will we owe him? "That's okay, Tía, if you want to go to Nice, we can rent our own chateau. We don't even know Dorian."

Dorian ignores my comment and thanks my aunt for the food. Maria calls me over to the pantry and shoves a mango protein smoothie in my hands.

"I really like him, Dulce. He's so cultured and worldly. And his family is from English nobility. Not like that Sebastian, who comes from *nada.*"

I give her a dirty look. "Why can't you just leave Sebastian alone?" Maria's so pretentious. She seems to forget that she came from nothing. She grew up picking strawberries in Gilroy but never talks about her past.

"I don't like his family. That mother of his—she never takes him to church, and she has all those candles and herbs in her home, claiming to be a curandera. She is up to no good!"

"She's a massage therapist and herbalist. Not a *bruja*!"

Maria thumbs her rosary beads. "She's evil, Dulce."

I shoo her from the room so I can talk to Dorian alone.

I pause to take a sip of my smoothie and look out my bay window onto the driveway. The Lotus that I thought Dorian had rented has a new car registration sticker in the window. Guess he's planning to stay around Marin for a while.

"Let's go outside," I motion to Dorian.

With my drink in one hand, I scoop up Salsa in the other. Dorian opens the screen door, and he follows me onto my redwood deck. I relax on my teak wood chaise and place my drink in the holder.

Dorian sits down on the chaise next to me. "That's some dog you got there."

"Yeah, she's got issues. I found her at the Hawaiian Humane Society when I was filming a movie. They wanted to put her to sleep because she had such severe mange, but I begged them to let me adopt her."

Salsa growls at him and then for the first time ever, she bites me.

"Salsa, no!"

What in the world? "Sorry, she never does that. I don't know what's gotten into her. She's a little crazy but isn't she beautiful?

"Sure, she is." Dorian grimaces. Salsa doesn't seem to be fond of immortal beings. She loves Sebastian, though maybe that's because he always brings her peanut butter treats. "So, how've you been coping?"

74

"Good. I don't ever have to do my hair and makeup anymore. What's not to love?"

He takes a big sip of his drink. "It's not all fun and games. Where's your picture? You must never let it out of your sight."

He's a total downer, but I can't stop staring at him. His violet eyes hypnotize me. "It's safe in my purse."

"That's good. But remember, Dulce, don't let anyone know our secret. Ever. And be careful. You can't be burning your face or drawing attention to yourself. You will be in danger."

I press my lips flat. "How did you know I burnt my face? Did you see me? Am I going to be able to start seeing things to?" The second those words left my lips, I realized something. I had my first vision on the night of the curse. And since then, I've had intense dreams every night. Was this a new power?

He ignores my question and continues to nag me. "I don't think you get it. Enjoy the time you have left with your family and friends. You think they aren't going to notice that you will look sixteen forever? Don't you understand the consequences?"

I gaze up at the sky and take a deep breath.

"I *can* handle this. I've read your book. I'm not going to throw my life away and become addicted to drugs and sex. I've never tried any drugs—or sex for that matter. Hell, I've never even been drunk. And I'm definitely not going to murder anyone. I'm not like you."

He abruptly gets off the chaise and then steps away from me. After pacing for a few seconds, he leans against the patio railing, studying my beloved bridges in the distance through the fog. "You're wrong, Dulce. You're just like me, and just like me, you'll stay young while everyone else grows old around you. You'll have to leave everyone you love, just like I had to. It's awful. And lonely, and I don't think you really understand the consequences of what will happen if you aren't careful."

My mouth can't even form the words to respond.

The silence is awkward for a second.

"I'll never be like you," I say under my breath. "And besides, this isn't the nineteenth century. I can blame my agelessness on plastic surgery. Look at Ryan Seacrest. He still looks like he is twenty."

"You know it's not that easy."

"Why can't it be?"

He comes closer to me and touches my face, his cold hand reminding me that he is not some normal teenage boy. "Dulce—"

"No! Don't touch me. I don't need some stupid pat on the back from you. I'm tired of people patting me on the back with one hand and stabbing me in the back with the other. I'm tired of everyone else saying what my next job will be, where I have to go each day, what I have to do. Finally, I'm in control. Me. I have the perfect body, and now I say what my next job is. I finally have some power—"

"You have traded your mom and friends, even Sebastian, for that power."

"Dammit, Dorian!" I leap up and throw my glass over the rail. It shatters on a towering oak tree in the backyard.

"That's it, Dulce!" he proclaims, taking out another tree with his own glass. "Scream. Break things. Take your anger out on me." Then his voice softens. He puts his hand on my shoulder.

This time I don't knock it away.

"Enjoy the perks while you can. When you can't hide anymore, I'll take you away. You will never be alone like I was."

I turn toward him, staring deep into his eyes. Here I was already being selfish. Immune to Dorian's pain. I study his soulless eyes—they're haunted and melancholy. One hundred and thirty years alone must've caused him to be so lonely. "Dorian, I want you to know that I believe you. Everything you've said. My soul knows you aren't lying to me."

His lips quiver. "You no longer have a soul." He hugs me as the world's most beautiful bridges vanish beneath the blanket of fog.

THE FRIENDSHIP

*Laughter is not at all a bad beginning for a **friendship**, and it is far the best ending for one.*

— OSCAR WILDE, THE PICTURE OF DORIAN GRAY

My driver's car hugs the curves of the road. Despite relaxing in the back of a cushy limo, I want to vomit. As beautiful as Stinson Beach is, I hate the treacherous and winding roads.

Once we arrive in town, the normally calming view of the ocean does little to alleviate my stress. This will be the first time since the spell that I've seen all the members of my cast.

The shoot is on the beach, which is currently completely deserted. I scan the scenery for Sebastian but don't see him. Instead, I spy Halia standing under a makeup canopy, with Vikki, Marcilla, and Asha huddled behind her.

But before I can say hi, I spot Eva. She pulls me into a chair inside the canopy. "You're late."

"Not really. My mom already hired someone to do my hair and makeup," I lie.

"I knew she was trying to replace me. But this is a beach shoot. They want a surfer girl vibe." She reaches for the curling iron, and I panic.

"What in the world?" Eva's mouth drops when my tightly coiled lock of hair straightens when she releases it from the barrel. Just like my experiment earlier, my hair rebels against the iron. Only this time, I have an audience.

Vikki points at my head. "Did you see that? It looks like she just used a flat iron."

"Yeah," shrugs Marcilla. "Must be *some* straightening treatment."

"Fine, Dulce. Tell your mom that I'm still your stylist and I'm under contract. She can't get rid of me that easily. And next time, don't put so much Moroccan Oil in your hair that it won't hold a curl!" Even Eva's flip-flops sound angry as she walks away.

Halia eyeballs me. She has to know something isn't right. My mind races—what should I tell her if she asks?

She sits down next to me, squeezes my hand. "Dulce, what's really going on?" She reaches into her bag and picks up a copy of *People*, which has a before and after picture of me on the cover.

I want to tell her the truth. She's my only girlfriend, and I don't want to lie to her, but I remember Dorian's warning and shrug my shoulder instead. Thankfully she lets it drop. "Are you coming to Sebastian's play and his cast party? Please? We're not a pentacle without you. Just a square."

"Not true. You guys could be a parallelogram," I say.

Vikki flops down on a blanket in the sand. "Yeah come," she says rolling her eyes up from her iPhone. "If you don't, everyone's just going to interrogate us all night about your Botox addiction." Marcilla and Asha laugh.

I glare at Vikki. She's so snarky that I sometimes forget how beautiful she is. Flawless mahogany skin without casting a single spell. "As much as I'd like to come so I can detract the reporters and free up your schedules so you all can flirt with everyone there, I'm going to have to pass." I have to stay at home tonight and reread *The Picture of Dorian Gray* so I can try to figure out ways to avoid my fate.

"Okay, your loss. Sebastian is supposed to be brilliant. Don't worry —I'll make sure to entertain him." Asha puckers up her plump lips. I want to smack her but comfort myself by knowing that Sebastian never goes for the tall, skinny girls.

Then again, I'm now skinny.

Marcilla, Vikki, and Asha each take one last look in my mirror. "You coming? We have to change into our swimsuits," Vikki says to Halia.

"Nah, I'm going to stay here with Dulce. I already have my bikini on under this dress."

"Whatever," says Vikki, and they walk through the sheer curtains and take a left near the lagoon.

Halia pulls on the edge of my dress. "They're gone. So, you have to tell me. Your skin, hair, and eyes look so great. Nobody believes the official story. And what's going on with you and Dorian? When Sebastian saw the picture in *Life & Style,* he ripped it up."

I figured Sebastian would be pissed. I'll deal with him later, but I can't bear to keep this secret from Halia any longer. "I saw Dorian today. But we are just friends. I do have to tell you something." I reach into my bag and take out *The Book of Shadows.* "I took home *The Book of Shadows* accidentally one night. Anyway, Winter chewed it up in the trailer before the shoot. I was freaking out, so I put the cover on this anthology that my tutor gave me. And after we did that everlasting youth spell—I was transformed."

Halia just stares at me, blank. After a minute, she laughs. "Oh, I get it. Hysterical. I bet we could totally sell that story to *The Sun.* They love stuff like that. So, seriously, who did your Botox? Will he work on me? My mom's not cool like your aunt—she will never sign a release for me."

"Just get emancipated like I did and you can do what you want."

Her face contorts. "Yeah, I need to, but I don't want to hurt my mom's feelings. So spill, girl."

I didn't expect her to believe me right away, so I keep talking. "Anyway, listen, I'm serious. I had the book open to *The Picture of Dorian Gray*. You know, by Oscar Wilde?"

Another blank stare.

"It's a story about a man who makes a wish to look like a portrait of himself and he stays the same age as the picture ages. Actually, it's about Dorian!"

"What?" Halia's cheeks flush. "It's cool. If you don't want to tell me your doctor's name, I understand."

"I'll prove it." I flip through the anthology open to my *Teen Glam* picture. "Look at this picture—see the zit, the frizzy hair, the dull, shoe polish color eyes, a mark on my cheek from the hair curler? That's the real me. I became the picture. I don't understand it either."

Halia studies the photo closely.

"Come on, girl. That's like the original proof of the picture, right? Before all the airbrushing? And really fabumazing makeup. Eva's an artist."

What am I thinking? Of course, she isn't just going to believe me. I need to do something drastic.

My eyes scan the canopy. The shiny blades from Eva's scissors beckon me. Without a second thought, I gouge the edge into my palm. An intense throbbing radiates down my fingers, and I hold back a scream.

"Duls, stop, are you insane? What the hell is wrong with you?"

I hold my hand up, so she doesn't miss it. "Watch."

Her eyelashes flutter, but as I stare into her eyes, I can see her pupils widen as I feel the droplets of blood dry up. Then, I shove the picture at her.

"Look at my hand."

Halia fondles the picture, tilting it this way and that so she can get a better angle. She looks at me, then the picture, but doesn't utter a sound.

"I don't know what's going on, Duls." Her expression shifts a little more with each time her eyes flick between my palm and the picture. Her eyes widen a bit and a smile tugs at her lips.

Halia believes me.

"Oh my god! You're a freak!"

"For sure." I slump into the sand. Having someone believe me besides Dorian makes me feel lighter.

Halia dances around me. "But this is so awesomesauce! You're going to look fabulous forever."

"I know, right? I never have to do my hair and makeup again, and Savvy definitely won't fire me."

She blinks hard. "Wait, are you trying to tell me your Dorian is *the* Dorian? He's like immortal? Man, the coolest guys always like you."

I hadn't wanted to reveal Dorian's identity to her, or to anyone for that matter. But I figure I've gone too far to turn back now.

"He says he is. I know I shouldn't believe him, but I can't help myself. For some reason, I just trust him."

She turns to his book in the anthology and points to a full-color illustration. "It does look just like him."

I hadn't really studied the illustration since I'd met Dorian, but the drawing is a mirror image. His hair is the same length as it is now and he's dressed in an old-school brown tuxedo complete with a bow tie, a vest, and tails. His eyes are the exact same color, and his smile is still crooked.

"Yeah, I think it is him."

She begins to thumb through the book, her fingers frenzied as her cheeks stretch into a grin. "Who should I be?"

Oh hell no! I should've never have told her the truth. Why didn't I listen to Dorian? "I don't think so. You have this all wrong! This is so not a good thing. I wish I could go back into time and never have done that spell."

Before I can say anything and pull the book away from her, she presses her lips.

"Don't be selfish, Dulce. You got glowing skin and hair. Hey, are there any vampires in here?"

I can't believe she's reacting so selfishly. For once, this is about me not her.

"One. She's actually in my favorite novella ever. *Carmilla* by J. Sheridan Le Fanu. She's a super cool vampire who falls in love with this girl named Laura."

Halia flips the page. "Let's save her for Marci."

Marcilla has a serious girlfriend from another *Savvy* show. The executives had made them keep their relationship a secret for a while, but then Savvy acted all fake and supportive during campaign season and had them film a public service announcement about LGBT youth.

"Vampires are totally played out anyway. You can send them off into twilight as far as I'm concerned. But I wouldn't mind disappearing too. I wish I could hang out without anyone noticing me. Is there a book like that?"

My heart drops. Of course, Halia wants to be invisible. I've already had a vision of her vanishing, and she has mentioned having a similar vision herself. Should I warn her? I lower my voice. "*The Invisible Man*. Not Ralph Ellison's version, though I love that book, but the one by Robert Louis Stevenson. Great book. You should read it."

"No need. You can read it for me and tell me what happens. I'm so excited! I won't have to deal with the paparazzi." Her glare has an impatient edge to it that I've never seen before.

"This isn't a joke, Halia. Dorian has been telling me stuff. Honestly, I'm scared."

Halia doesn't even look up from the anthology. She's thumbing through *Invisible Man*—no doubt plotting how sneaky she can be if she were invisible. I have to admit that anonymity would be nice. I should've said my spell over *that* book.

She finally shuts the book. "Relax, Duls, we can work this out, it's not so bad. We can always try to reverse it. Let me know when, and I can gather the girls."

She hugs me, and I bury my head on her shoulder. Maybe she's right, and this isn't a bad thing. I just have to be careful and stay in control.

We separate, and she looks up at me. "But you're going to that play with me tonight."

THE ROMANCE

When one is in love, one always begins by deceiving one's self, and one always ends by deceiving others. That is what the world calls a **romance.**

— OSCAR WILDE, THE PICTURE OF DORIAN GRAY

CHAPTER 8

My driver drops me off at the theater at my high school, Redwood, in Larkspur. It's Shakespeare week, and Sebastian is playing Romeo.

The girls had all gone to Asha's house to get ready, but since my hair and makeup won't change, I just drove myself.

The other girls emerge from the limo and walk toward the theater. I join them on the red carpet the school has put out. Redwood is using Sebastian's starring role to raise funds for its theater program, hence the pressure on the full cast to show up.

A reporter from the school paper, *The Bark*, approaches me. "Dulce, what do you say about the rumors that you've had an extreme makeover?"

"They aren't true, but tonight I won't answer any more questions about myself. I'm here to support my friend, Sebastian Vasquez."

"Friend? Isn't Sebastian your boyfriend? Or did he break up with you when you cheated on him with that mystery man you've been photographed with?"

I push past him, accidentally on purpose knocking over his recorder with my shoulder. We make our way over to some fans. I flash smile after smile, sign autographs, and head into the theater. Sebastian is the only member of our cast who really loves to act. He's devoted himself completely to his craft, always performing with the Marin Shakespeare Company during our summer break. I personally think he's nuts. Though the entire cast attends Redwood at least once a week, the girls and I complete most of our classes through independent study. Not Sebastian. He attends real classes as often as his schedule allows and dedicates all of his free time to Redwood's theater company. He directs plays, does improvisation, stage-manages, and practices live theater for hours. He's like a mini James Franco. Sebastian is determined to win the Academy Award for Best Actor one day. Kinda cool.

The front row is filled with Sebastian's fangirls. They've coined themselves "The Covettes." I used to think they all hated me because I play his girlfriend on the show, but now I believe they'd rather we were together to make the romance of the show real. I'm no longer threatened by their jealousy.

The lights dim. Halia sits next to me and squeezes my hand. "Showtime."

I relax into my seat.

Sebastian takes the stage, and the girls scream. When their shrills die down, he says his first line. "Is the day so young?"

The orange glow from the stage lights shines on him. His glossy black hair is slicked back, and his dimples seem to be magnified.

But I don't see Sebastian. I see Romeo—Sebastian has completely transformed into a Montague. Street savvy *Joaquin—The White-lighter,* has vanished before my eyes.

Has he always been this talented and I have just never bothered to notice?

His pronunciation and diction are perfect. He even makes iambic pentameter sound sexy.

Dammit, why didn't I audition to be Juliet?

"Halia, isn't Sebastian amazing?" I whisper.

She knocks back some Reece's Pieces. "I guess. Same as he always is."

But I hang on his every word. What if Dorian's right and my time with my family and friends is short? I need to embrace life to the fullest. No more waiting for the right moment to profess my feelings to Sebastian. It's now or never.

When the play ends, I jump out of my seat and applaud.

Halia pulls me away walks over to the other girls. "So, are we all gonna go to that party in Ross?"

I pause. I need some time alone with Sebastian. "Yeah, I'll catch up with you guys in a bit. I'll give Sebastian a ride."

"Wouldn't he like that?" Vikki eyes me hard. "Whatever. See you there."

I leave the theater and sit on the edge of one of the planter boxes outside the lobby. I'm not there long before Sebastian emerges and his fans flock to him. Tweens pull out their autograph books, give him teddy bears, and I think one poor girl even faints.

I pretend to be patient, but inside, my chest burns. All these girls, these beautiful girls would do anything to be with their teen idol. Have I squandered any chance with Sebastian?

"Dulce."

My heart beats rapidly, and my palms sweat. It's Dorian! Why is he here trying to ruin my night? I stand up, tug on his shirt and pull him toward the side of the building, praying that Sebastian doesn't see us.

"What are you doing here? Are you following me? You're like a complete stalker."

His lips are trembling. "Dulce, please listen to me. Sebastian, he's just like Sibyl. I saw him act tonight. He was great. But he's not right for you. Come away with me tonight."

Who does this jerk think he is? I grind my teeth. "Look, Dorian, you don't own me. I'm not your girlfriend. Just go back to whatever book you crawled from and leave Sebastian and me alone."

His eyes widen, and the vein in his neck strains against his skin. "You're mine, Dulce. If you love Sebastian, you will leave him alone."

Mine? I've only met him three times, and now I'm his? He's so gorgeous, but why is he so desperate?

But I know the answer to this question. He is desperate because he has outgrown his lovers. A constant revolving door.

I believe in true love. My one person. Like a lobster mating for life.

But unfortunately, I hope that person is Sebastian, not Dorian.

I try to think of what to say to him, but I'm unable to speak. For the first time since I've met him, I want to get as far away from him as possible. But I've told him too much. He knows my secret. He could expose me. He could ruin me.

Over my shoulder, I see Sebastian taking pictures with his fans. I turn back to Dorian. "Hey, I'm sorry. I've just been stressed out with the curse and all. Do you want to come to this party? It's in Ross."

He smoothens his shorts. "I can't. But please, promise me you'll be careful. You aren't in control of your emotions. If anything happens to Sebastian, you'll never forgive yourself. Not even in one hundred and thirty years."

I study his pale face. This boy in front of me is clearly lonely and filled with regret. His eyes stare at me longingly, but I have no clue what he truly wants from me. Does he really want me to be his forever? He doesn't know me either. "I'll be careful. If you change your mind, the party is the second house on the right on Shady Lane."

"I won't change my mind. I'll text you later, and maybe we can meet up."

I nod, and he walks toward the parking lot. I return to the planter box to wait for Sebastian.

When the crowd dissolves, Sebastian comes over to me. I bite my fingernails, knowing any damage they suffer will be fixed within minutes.

"Hey, babe. Glad you could make it. What did you think?"

His straight black hair skims his eyebrows. Sebastian never makes me nervous, but for once, my tongue seems tangled. "I think . . . you're amazing."

He shuffles his feet. "Come on, Duls. Stop playing."

I straighten my shoulders. "I'm serious, Bas. You blew me away tonight. You are the perfect Romeo." I pause and decide to go for it. "I was jealous of Juliet."

Sebastian's lips part and his dimples deepen. "What are you saying, Duls? You always make fun of my, what was it, 'silly high school theater.'"

I never knew that he thought I was mocking him. "I'm sorry. I never meant it was stupid. I just didn't understand why you spend all your time acting. It's just a job for me. But you . . . you completely lose yourself in it. I respect that."

"Yeah?" He bends so he's closer to me and pushes back a lock of my hair, his finger tracing the curves of my face.

I want to tell him everything—my feelings about him, my worries about the curse, my fears about Dorian. My hands shake. Will he believe me? Even Halia was focused more on using the spell for herself. Only Dorian understands me. Could he be right about me putting Sebastian in danger?

I read the book. I know Sybil dies.

I will never forgive myself if something happens to Sebastian

Sebastian places his hand on my face. "Let's get out of here."

THE PASSION

*I want to make Romeo jealous. I want the dead lovers of the world to hear our laughter, and grow sad. I want a breath of our **passion** to stir dust into consciousness, to wake their ashes into pain.*

— OSCAR WILDE, THE PICTURE OF DORIAN GRAY

CHAPTER 9

The Branson Lacrosse team is holding one of their ragers at the captain's parents' house. The music from the DJ roars down an otherwise quiet street in Ross. Normally, I would hate this scene. But tonight, I just want to cut loose.

Sebastian and I walk in, and I scan the room. Everyone is staring at us, but I pretend not to notice.

A gorgeous preppy boy winks at me. "So what can I get you guys?"

Sebastian places his hand on my back. "I'll have a beer and Dulce will have a cola."

My heart beats fast. "Make it two beers."

Sebastian's eyes bulge. "Duls. You never drink. You sure?"

Why is everyone telling me what to do? "Yeah, I'm sure. It's just a drink."

"Relax. I didn't mean anything. It's just . . . I don't know, weird. First, you act all into me—now you want to drink. Just doesn't seem like you."

I'm a new person. The old Dulce is dead. "You drink all the time, Sebastian. And that's not all you do—I've seen you get high. Why is everyone on my case? You, Maria, Rosa, Dorian, even Halia. I don't need a babysitter."

Cute, preppy boy returns with the beer. I take a swig and check him out. Tall, tan, blond hair, green eyes. Not my type, but what the hell? "So, what's your name?"

"Geoff. You want to go outside?"

Anything to get away from Sebastian. From Dorian. From my curse. From the mess that is my life. "Sure, Geoff." He takes my arm, and I leave Sebastian standing there in the kitchen, his mouth open.

Geoff leads me to the deck overlooking an old English-style garden. A couple is making out on a chaise lounge chair. A few boys are hunched in a corner; one is holding a mirror in his hand and snorting coke with a dollar bill. I'm pretty sure a girl is puking in the bushes. Gross. Parties have never been my scene. Before this spell, I knew who I was and what I wanted. I'd worked way too hard and sacrificed too much to screw up my reputation with one debaucherous night. But now, my world seems different.

Geoff stands in my space; his pupils seem dilated, but maybe that's the moonlight. His soft blond curls frame his face. "It's awesome you showed up. I see your costars a lot, but you never come to these parties. What gives?"

I don't want to talk to this guy. I just want to forget my problems. "It's just not my thing." I take a long drink of my beer. It's gross, like a combination of soap, stale wheat bread, and a *Jarritos Toronja* grapefruit soda.

Before I get a chance to come to my senses and find Sebastian, Geoff grabs me. His arms slide down my back, pulling my waist into his.

His beer-spiked breath blows hot on my neck. Oh no. This is not what I want. At all. Has this curse caused me to lose my mind as well?

I try to push him off me, but apparently, strength is not one of my new powers. I struggle in his embrace, wanting to flee.

"Get off her!" Sebastian's voice rings out.

Geoff pulls back before his lips touch mine. "What's it to you, pretty boy? Back up."

"Dulce, what the hell is going on?" Sebastian's jaw is clenched, and he has that look he gets on the set when he is battling warlocks. He's pissed. Not that I can blame him. I'm being a bitch.

I feel so dirty. "I'm sorry, Geoff. I have to go." I dash back into the house, past Halia and the girls, and leave the party.

Sebastian is in pursuit. "Duls, wait."

I run down Shady Lane and slump on the side of Sebastian's truck. The passenger side opens, and I climb in and Sebastian slides in next to me.

"What's gotten into you? First, you don't return my messages and calls. I see pictures of you in the mags with this British dude. Old friend, my ass. I've known you for years, and you've never mentioned him. You show up at my play and are acting all flirty with me, making me think maybe I finally have a shot. And now you ditch me to hook up with some random guy? Why are you playing all these bullshit games with me?"

Have a chance? He actually wants me? Probably only because now I'm finally hot.

"I don't know." I sigh and lean my head against the steering wheel for a second before looking back at him. "I'm sorry. I'm just going through something now." I turn away from him. My mind keeps replaying how awful I just behaved. I hate myself.

He touches my arm. "Man, you're cold. Here."

Sebastian takes his jacket off and drapes it around my shoulders. His hand rests on the back of my neck. Though his jacket is lined with fleece, my skin remains as cold as my iced mochas.

"You sick, Duls?"

I push his hand away so he can't feel my frosty skin. "No. I'm good."

"You sure? Your skin is cold, and you're acting weird. You never want to go to parties, and you're drinking and making out with a guy you don't even know? The only thing you ever want to do is go to those stupid foreign movies with those subtitles and attend book readings. What's up?"

He can't possibly understand, and I don't want to sound like a freak. And even if he does believe me, what if Dorian was right? Am I doomed to a life of loneliness and heartache?

Or worse yet, what if I hurt Sebastian?

"Nothing, okay? I'm just stressed about the tabloids and contracts and restrictions. I'm sick of being a Mary Jane."

Sebastian whispers into my ear. "Don't shut me out."

He puts his arm around me, and I melt when I see his dimples. He's so different from Dorian. Sweet, cute, and real.

"Will you talk to me? Tell me what's going on? You say it's stress, but who is this guy you've been seen with? Did Rosa organize this so your contract will get renewed? To create buzz? I know you, Dulce. At least I thought I did. You'd never sell out for publicity. Is he the one who got you the Botox?"

"Sebastian, I can explain, but this is so much bigger than you could imagine."

"I just need to know if there's something between you and this Dorian . . . because . . . because I don't think—"

"Bas, please . . . don't."

He slumps in the seat. "Fine. That's okay. I get it."

"No, you don't. You're getting the wrong idea."

"It's okay. I get it. I mean, you and I are friends. Really good friends."

There is no way I'm going to lie to him. But I'm not sure how Sebastian is going to handle my story.

I hold his hand. His skin is dark and warm, unlike Dorian's. "I will tell you everything, but you have to believe me. I would never lie to you."

He nods to me.

I take a deep breath. "Sebastian, I cast a spell, and it made me beautiful, and I can never die."

"Uh, what?"

I tell him the full story and show him my magazine picture.

He studies it closely and then traces my face with his fingers.

"You never had surgery?"

"Of course not. You know I don't believe in that stuff."

He looks back at the picture and then at me.

He remains quiet, alternating his gaze between the picture and my face.

"Oh man, this kind of stuff is not possible. Come on, Duls . . ."

I clutch his wrist, trying to convince him to believe me. "Sebastian, I am not insane. I wouldn't make this up."

"Well, I believe that you believe what you're saying—"

"Sebastian, I know what your family believes. You always said you believed in that kind of stuff too. And now, what, because it's actually happening, you're going to question it?"

"Duls, my mom treats people for stupid stuff like bad air. She grinds some herbs, cuts up some pantyhose, and prays to Saint Rita. Sure, everyone says they feel better, but it's probably just been the power of suggestion—positive thinking. It works, but the point is, it isn't anything crazy like you saying you're eternally beautiful. Immortal. Turning into one of the characters from those Twilight movies."

"Those were vampires, Bas. I don't thirst for blood. I just have good hair. No zits."

He doesn't respond. I stare up at the tree-lined street. It's so calm here, so serene. For the first time in what feels like forever, I wish for a moment that Sebastian and I could just be two normal teenagers sitting together in a truck. I don't want the television show, paparazzi, or spells. What would our life be like?

His silence makes me panicky, so I throw in a buffer to try to make things less weird. "I want you to know I'm not seeing Dorian. Obviously, you saw the pictures, but you have to know they were taken out of context."

Sebastian doesn't look at me. "You know I never believe that stuff. It's so stupid." I can tell he's confused but trying hard not to show it. "How do you know him?"

"He's not an old family friend. That's a lie Rosa made up. I met him after I woke up at the hospital. But he told me the same curse thing happened to him."

His mouth drops. "Seriously? You are so naïve—some weird English dude shows up at the hospital that you're in and you believe that he suffered some spell?"

"I'm not gullible. Have you ever read *The Picture of Dorian Gray*? Dorian is the character from the book." I have to admit that sounds as crazy as my curse story.

"Sure, he is." He smirks in disbelief. "At least he's original. Great cover story for a stalker. A character from a stupid book."

"It's actually an amazing book. Wilde was brilliant." I know I'm not helping matters.

Sebastian can't even look at me anymore. "I need to meet him."

I lower my voice to a whisper. "Well, that won't be too hard. I can invite him to the set."

He pulls out his iPhone and starts texting. "I'm going to figure out who this guy is. My cousin's a cop."

I like how protective he is being of me, but I don't want him getting involved. I take his phone from him and run my fingers on his arm, letting my hand relax on his leg.

He leans into me. Is he going to kiss me?

This wouldn't be our first kiss. But this time there is no audience. There's no director telling Sebastian where to put his hands or telling me to tilt my head a little more to the right.

Anticipation, excitement, and nerves fill my body. I've dreamt of this moment for years, fantasizing about every scenario in which this could possibly happen.

And it's happening now.

I close my eyes as his lips cover mine. Soft at first, like our lips want to savor their first encounter that has been dictated by our hearts and not our scripts.

I throw my arms around his neck, pulling him into me as the stubble on his chin grazes my skin. His hands grasp my hair, and he kisses me deeper.

I kiss him back. Our mouths meet and his tongue probes my mouth. A bolt of pleasure surges through my body. How many nights have I dreamt about this kiss, dreamt about him?

All my dreams were finally coming true.

We have broken the line we said we would never cross, and I don't care what it means. Sebastian's lips have made me forget Dorian, my curse, my show, my mom, my life, if only for a moment.

"I'm crazy about you, Dulce."

I want to tell him how connected I feel to him. Before this stupid spell, he was all I thought about and the only one in the world I could trust. But how can I start something with him when I will have to leave him forever in a few years?

"I'm crazy about you too, but I'm scared. Things are so confusing with this curse."

He bites his lip, and at that moment, I know he doesn't believe me. "Yeah, okay. I see."

"I'm going to be sixteen forever! Don't you get it? There's no turning back for me. People are going to start to notice. And I'm going to have to leave all of my friends and family behind and go into hiding. At least that's what Dorian is saying. I mean, it almost makes sense. I'm doomed—he's doomed. And I can't imagine ever leaving you. This will just make it harder than it is."

He pulls away from me. "How do you know all of this? Say I believe all this . . . how do you even know that's it's not temporary?"

"Well Dorian said—"

"Ahh. Okay. It is about this guy. You trust him over me?"

"Absolutely not, but he knows things . . . things I never told him. He says he can help me."

"Sure he can. Look, Duls, I don't know about your curse or anything, but we can find a way to break it. I'm a whitelighter remember?" He makes his stupid whitelighter hand sign.

I laugh. He always knows how to lighten the mood. But I know he's just playing with me. He isn't taking this seriously. "I just—" I press my lips together, searching for the right words. "I just want to get a handle on what is happening to me before I complicate matters. You mean the world to me, you know that. I just need a little time to adjust."

Sebastian hunches his shoulders. "Don't play games with me. I'm not gonna be here if you mess around with Dorian. You don't know anything about him. He's not who he says he is."

Sebastian is right. I don't know anything about Dorian. But for some reason, I believe everything he has said to me, even if I'm not heeding his warnings. I told Halia. Now I've told Sebastian.

"Duls, I've wanted you forever," he whispers into my ear.

The only problem is Sebastian has no idea how long my new forever might be.

THE SENSATION

*Live! Live the wonderful life that is in you! Let nothing be lost upon you. Be always searching for new **sensations**. Be afraid of nothing.*

— OSCAR WILDE, THE PICTURE OF DORIAN GRAY

CHAPTER 10

Sebastian drives me home after our long talk in his truck. He leans into me, and I can feel his breath on my neck. Is he going to kiss me again?

He cups my face in his hands and gives me another kiss. This kiss was different than the one earlier tonight. Softer, more loving, more intimate.

"Will you be my girlfriend?"

Girlfriend? I want to scream yes! yes! and ay, Dios mío, yes! But something holds me back.

Why did he never ask me to be his girlfriend before my curse? Before I was perfect. Does he like me or just the way I look?

I have to know.

"Why did you never ask me out before?"

He wrings his hands. "You've always blown hot and cold with me. Like you are doing now. But tonight, for the first time, I really feel it. I know you want me like I want you."

How stupid have I been? I guess I have been giving him mixed signals. But I've always wanted him—I just didn't want to be rejected. "I want to say yes so bad, but I need time."

His hands drop from my face, and his shoulders slump. "Why? I thought you liked me."

I nod. "I do. I do. I'm just kind of a mess. I'll tell you tomorrow. I just need . . . I need a handle of some stuff. This isn't about how much I like you. This is about the curse."

His face contorts to an annoyed smirk. "Whatever. Night."

Wow. That was weird. I probably hurt his feelings. I exit the truck and my phone beeps. A text from Dorian.

Dorian: Come out with me. I need to see you. It's urgent.

Dulce: It's eleven. I have to work tomorrow.

Dorian: I'll pick you up in five minutes.

Damn, didn't I just say no? But the truth is, I want to see him. I need to see him. Maybe seeing him will help clear up the confusion I have about Sebastian.

I don't even bother to text my aunt. Not only am I emancipated, but she thinks that I'm at the party still. I doubt she's watching me from the window waiting for me to come home.

She's not my mother.

I appreciate the freedom, but sometimes I wonder what it would be like to have someone worry about me, love me with no financial incentive, forbid me from doing something out of concern.

I guess I'll never know.

Dorian pulls into my driveway. I attempt to open the car door, but before I can blink, he puts the brakes on and exited to open the car door for me. Such a gentleman.

"You look radiant tonight, Dulce."

His face comes to focus, and his beauty stuns me. Sebastian is hot, but Dorian is classically handsome. I can't help but feel drawn to him, torn between my desire for both of these guys. Just a few weeks ago, as Halia had pointed out, I was super single. But now for once in my life, I have options.

And I like it.

"So, where are we going?"

"To the city. I'm going to wow you."

His car travels toward the glorious Golden Gate bridge. Crossing to San Francisco never ceases to amaze me. One look at the lights and my heart is filled with excitement. Leaving Marin makes me feel like I'm leaving my childhood behind, tempted by the thrill of the city.

Dorian navigates San Francisco's curvy streets with ease, and I can't help but wonder how this sexy man trapped in a boy's body would navigate my curves. His hand expertly clutches the stick shift and the heat pools in my body.

He turns onto Sansome Street and valets the car at The Stock Exchange Tower. Ugh, boring.

"What are we doing here? Isn't this place for old people?"

His face drops. Oh, shoot.

"You mean, like me?"

"No, not at all. Just never been anywhere like here before."

He takes my hand and whispers in my ear, "Let me impress you."

He flashes his ID at the doorman and leads me into this luxurious building. We take the elevator to the tenth floor, and when the doors open, my mouth drops. The City Club of San Francisco. I'm greeted by a grand ornate staircase that features brass figurines.

Dorian kisses my hand. "Look up, sweetheart."

And up I do. There in front of me is the most breathtaking mural I have ever seen. I drop Dorian's hand and run to the top of the red velvet covered stairs. There is a lady with dark hair and blue eyes clutching fruit with a boy under her clutching an airplane.

I don't even have to ask. I know my art history. This is a Diego Rivera.

"Is this for real?"

"Yup. It's the Allegory of California. Diego painted it in the 1930s."

I'm literally speechless. Seeing my favorite artist come alive in front of me, not seeing a picture of it in some book, awakes a hunger inside me. A hunger for knowledge.

And I realize that if I date Dorian, he can truly show me the world unlike anyone else can.

After marveling at the mural, Dorian takes me into a private members' only room.

The lounge is dim, but I focus on the view of the entire city. The towering TransAmerica building with Alcatraz in the distance.

My stomach is in knots. I know I shouldn't be here, but I'm having a blast.

"We'll have two Dorian Grays." Dorian hands the cocktail waitress two IDs and whispers in her ear. She giggles and goes to get our drinks.

"Dorian Grays? You have a drink named after you? What's in it? Equal parts arrogance and vanity?"

His violet eyes twinkle with amusement. "Actually, the cocktail was created in 1999 at the Lobby Bar in One Aldwych, London. It's Rum, Grand Marnier, orange and cranberry juice. It's quite delightful. You'll love it."

"I doubt it. And I'm only sixteen. We're not at some teen party. Whose ID did you give her? And what about you? You're only seventeen anyway, I mean, officially. Or unofficially. You know what I mean."

"Please, I've been alive for over a hundred years, and you think I don't have an ID? I have several in fact. And I recently had yours made."

He flashes me a completely legitimate Mississippi driver's license with my picture on it and the name Dulce Gray in black ink.

Dulce Gray?

I fondle my ID. "Cute, Dorian. What am I, your sister? No one would believe I'm twenty-one, especially now, since I look like I'm a tween. Plus, I'm a celebrity. People know who I am."

Dorian lets out a laugh, and his hand clutches my thigh. "Sister, hardly. I was thinking teenage bride."

"I get it—bride of Frankenstein, oh no, bride of Dorian Gray. Maybe there's a cocktail for that."

"You're cheeky. One of the many reasons I like you." The waitress brings us the drinks, and Dorian slips her a few bills before turning his attention back on me.

I relax into the velvet sofa and take the tiniest sip of my drink. Dorian is right—I love it. "So, why did you need to see me so urgently?"

Dorian knocks back his drink and stares deep into my eyes. "I'm a patient man, Dulce. So, I'm willing to wait out your childhood flirtation with Sebastian. It's adorable, really. But I just wanted to give you a glimpse of what your life will be like when you finally run away with me."

I sputter a bit, not sure if I'm offended or intrigued by his blatant remark. "Oh, *Mr.* Gray. I'm not going anywhere with you."

Dorian smirks and continues. "I have residences all over the world, a chateau on the Italian Riviera, an apartment in the 6th Arrondissement in Paris, a flat in Mayfair, a Brownstone in Boston. My investments have done quite well over the years."

My chest tightens. I have always dreamed of living in Paris.

Dorian senses my hesitation and sweetens the deal. "I know you love to read and study literature. You could attend the best universities in the world, Harvard, Oxford, The Sorbonne, Trinity College, and I will take care of all your expenses. And your family will never want for anything."

I run my hands through my hair. Fantasies of living abroad, surrounded by history, culture, art, and literature fill my head. "But I'd have to leave everyone behind, my family, Halia . . . Sebastian."

His cold hand turns icy. "Dulce, I'd give you everything you ever wanted. We could be so happy together. For eternity. And of course, what is mine would be yours, if you agreed."

"Agreed to what?"

He takes both my hands and nuzzles my neck. "Give me your picture, Dulce. And I will make you very happy."

I drop his hands and push him away. "Oh no. I've read your book. If you destroy my picture, I will die. You would control my life and death. No way."

Dorian licks his lips. "I'm not looking to control you—I'm just more experienced than you are. If your picture gets into the wrong hands, your life could be over. I want to protect you."

I don't need or want his protection. I just want to go home and call Sebastian. But I don't want to tell him that I'd snuck out to meet up with Dorian. My heart burns with guilt.

Then an idea strikes me.

"Where's your picture?"

"It's safe. In a lock box in Switzerland," he answers without hesitation.

"You're lying to me. You told me to keep my picture with me at all times. Why wouldn't you follow your own advice? If you want my picture, then I must have yours too. Fair is fair."

He speaks no words and reaches his arm around my waist. His hot breath smells of rum as he places his mouth over mine. My head tells me to push him off me.

But I don't.

I kiss him back, my tongue exploring his warm mouth as his hands rub up my thighs. Dorian is an experienced lover that knows how to satisfy a woman, not a young teenager figuring what makes a girl tick like Sebastian. I want to taste Dorian, for him to taste me. I want to feel every bit of pleasure that those lips promise my body.

I finally pull away from him.

He grins at me. "What are you doing this weekend?"

I pause, trying to regain my breath. "It's closing night of Sebastian's play, so I'm going to go and then we are going to the cast party."

His blinks hard. "Of course, it is. He's Romeo."

"I know what you're thinking—he's playing Romeo, and your Sybil was Juliet. But it's not like that. First of all, Sebastian's brilliant in it, so I'm not going to dump him because he sucks like she did. And even if I did, he's not stupid enough to poison himself over me."

Dorian's hands shake. He turns me toward him and pushes me up against the pillows. "Don't go to his play, Dulce. I'm serious. Don't make the same mistakes that I have."

I look at him, like really look at him, and see all the pain and sorrow that he has lurking deep inside him. "I'm not you, and Sebastian is not Sibyl. I am not going to make the same mistakes you did."

"You need to let him go and come with me. Please. It's the only way to be sure."

I take a moment and realize that Dorian could be right. We share the same curse; our lives are seemingly parallel. But knowledge is power. I adore Sebastian, despite my disloyal behavior with Dorian tonight. I'm not going to stop having feelings for Sebastian tomorrow night, even if he bombs in the play. I can protect myself and Sebastian.

But I have to agree with Dorian right now, or he won't let me go.

"Sure, let me go to the bathroom and freshen up."

He smiles, and I kiss his cheek.

I walk to the ladies' room, and when Dorian is no longer looking, I make a sharp left and dart down the fire escape.

Nothing is going to keep me from Sebastian—not a spell and certainly not Dorian.

Afraid to use the front door, I find another restroom on the ground floor. I take a deep breath, hoist myself up on the sink, and climb out the window, leaving Dorian behind.

THE SCANDAL

*I love **scandals** about other people, but scandals about myself don't interest me. They have not got the charm of novelty.*

— OSCAR WILDE, THE PICTURE OF DORIAN GRAY

CHAPTER 11

I wake up with a major headache, barely remembering the events of last night. For sure, I'm drained, but I always feel this way after parties. It doesn't last long, though. My stomach feels upset though. I hate myself for seeing Dorian behind Sebastian's back. But I needed to find out what Dorian wanted from me.

I am excited for the dress rehearsal of the *Quinceañera* episode, which *Teen Glam* magazine is covering. The rest of my coven will make up the *damas* in my court. All I care about is that Sebastian is my *chambelan*. After all, *Teen Glam* has recently anointed him "Hollywood's Hottest Hottie."

Despite the fears I expressed to him last night, I've made my decision. I want him. And, after all these years, I know that he wants me. Nothing will stop us from being together.

Seeing Dorian last night solidified my feelings for Sebastian. Sure, Dorian is sexy and sophisticated, but Sebastian has my heart.

I can't wait to tell him.

I slip into my stunning custom-made gown. The sunshine-shaded strapless, corset seamed bodice is decorated with sparkling embroidery, and the back ties up in lace. The tulle skirt is asymmetrically draped in many layers and edged with beads. Luckily, they just did the final fitting a few days ago, after the spell. I place the diamond-encrusted crown on my head and look into the mirror.

I walk into the kitchen. Maria eyes me up and down and then bites her lip. I wonder if she overheard me talking about the spell with Dorian when he came over that day, but she still hasn't confronted me about it. I think she has accepted that something strange is going on, but if she knew exactly what, she would probably think I was crazy. She's hardcore Catholic and already believes I am doing the work of *El Diablo* by starring in *The Coven*. But somehow, she excuses my dance with the devil as long as she sees dollar signs.

I grab Winter from his X-Pen and pet him. Maria waddles over to me with a disapproving glance.

"Ay, Dulce! I warned you about doing this . . . this show and acting like a *bruja*. I should have never let you bring that dirty *conejo* into this house."

Why take this out on Winter? He's the cleanest bunny. But he is the one who destroyed *The Book of Shadows*. Maybe Maria has a point?

"*Gracias a Dios* Padre Arturo is coming over today." She clutches the antique cross around her neck and says a prayer. She tells me to wait and then dashes off to her bedroom and returns holding a tiny box. "I was going to give this to you for your birthday, but you need it now."

I open the box and pull out my mother's antique pearl rosary. I clutch it to my heart, and a lump grows in my throat as I stare at the picture on my nightstand of my mom carrying it down the aisle when she married my father. "Thanks, Tía." I hug her.

She kisses me on the cheek. "You're welcome. She always wanted you to have it." In a rare display of emotion, Maria blinks back tears. "Since your hair and makeup are already done, go pray the rosary. And don't tell Padre Arturo about all this hocus-pocus mumbo jumbo you were saying in the hospital. He'd have a heart attack."

I obediently shuffle my feet over to my bed and nervously begin to pray to my rosary. Am I possessed? Will Padre Arturo take one look at me and try to exorcise me?

If so, he must stay away from me. No matter what.

Will my prayers break my spell? After a few Our Fathers, Hail Marys, Glory Be to the Father, I gently place my rosary on my nightstand and sprint back to the mirror, wondering if I will see my split ends in all their glory. But no, my hair is still as smooth and shiny as it was a few minutes ago.

Okay—I am still bewitched. Time to shoot!

"Dulce, your guests are here," Maria calls down the hall.

I stroll into our backyard, but if I hadn't just walked out of my own house, I wouldn't know where I was. Our deck has been trans-formed into a mini Disneyland. The actual Quince episode is going to be held at the real Disneyland, but since we are shooting up in Marin all month, the Savvy execs decided to throw the rehearsal in my home so we could soak up the Mexican vibes with my aunt's traditional Spanish style garden featuring a fountain and Mexican tiles. Always looking to enter the crossover Latin market, they hope to launch a line of *Quinceañera* dresses after they air the special, "Ria's *Quinceañera*." Mr. Mulberg told me to pick my favorite fairy tale as the theme for my Quince. I went with *Beauty and the Beast* because Belle loves reading as much as I do. Bookworms gotta stick together. So, the party planner went all out, and now my backyard looks like it is about to host the winter Olympics.

Dressed like the last czar, Mr. Mulberg runs over to me. "Dulce, you look fabulous! Finally, a dress that fits you right. Took costuming long enough." He snaps at the stylist to drape a jacket over me since I'm shivering. Ever since the spell, my body always thinks it's winter.

"Ooh," Mr. Mulberg says, his eyes roaming to the food table. "Is that your aunt's famous guacamole?" He doesn't wait for my answer before striding away from me and over to the table. I'm still looking after him, wondering why he seems so scattered, when the stylist drops a huge puffy coat over my shoulders.

"Thanks." I shove my arms into the sleeves and tuck my hands into the pockets. "Do you know if everyone else is here yet?"

"Yeah, they are over on the porch." She points to a group of people across the yard, and I spot Sebastian before heading in that direction.

"Hey," he says, smiling and looking every inch of the character he's supposed to be. My cheeks flush, and I resist the urge to run to a mirror to see if they actually changed color or just stayed the same rosy shade that was in the *Teen Glam* shot. "Sexy dress."

"I was about to say the same thing."

"I can't believe they hired a film crew for the rehearsal to pander to the Hispanic audience." Sebastian takes my hand and squeezes it. "I hate being used for Savvy's marketing demographics. At least I'm here with you."

"Don't you two look like the cutest couple ever?" Asha's shrill voice interrupts our moment. I turn around and see the rest of my "court" in a rainbow assortment of ball gowns. "Remember, honey—it's your fake fifteenth birthday party, not your wedding."

Sebastian whispers into my ear, "May not be your wedding, but we could practice for the wedding night."

I playfully slap him, and he kisses me on the cheek, then drops my hand and makes his way over to the other girls' dates.

"Dulce, you look totally gorgeous! Have you lost weight?" Vikki spins me around like a dreidel. "Maybe they won't fire you after all."

"What do you mean, 'after all'?"

Vikki just laughs and adjusts her snow white knit cap. "Nothing. It's just something I heard my agent saying."

Mr. Mulberg beckons us all to the middle of my backyard where a dance floor has been set up. "I'd like to welcome you all to Ria's Quince rehearsal. You all know Selena Lord, winner of *Dancing under the Stars*." All about the cross-promotion, Savvy will also use my Quince episode as an excuse to endorse their line of *Dancing under the Stars* ballroom DVDs, a product of their other hit series. Selena is going to teach my court the waltz. I'm super excited to meet her since she is also Latina and from Marin. She is so spunky and tiny, and the girl dances like a bolt lightning.

"*Bienvenidos*. Um. I'm super honored to be here and teach you the waltz. I never had a *Quinceañera* because I was competing, so I'm totally excited to help you out. Please stand behind me."

As we all fumble around on the steps, I notice how much easier it is to turn than it had been last time I danced. Maybe this spell has made me more graceful too. That would be awesome. I peek over at the boys' side to where Sebastian is bungling the steps and see him smile when he catches my glance. He is trying so hard which I find adorable.

"Dulce, I need to speak with you," Mr. Mulberg says, pulling me out of my lesson. When I don't move fast enough for him, he snaps his fingers. "Now, Dulce."

I move much faster and try really hard not to break an ankle as I exit over to the lawn to where he is standing away from everyone else. "I just want to say that I'm really happy that you've been taking our advice about your health. We never encourage our girls to diet, but you do look better, and your face is sparkling today. I've put a call into your agent with an offer to renew your contract for three seasons. And we are even talking about a solo spinoff—*Ria: The Good Witch*."

"Are you serious? Thank you!" I jump up and give him a big hug.

My own show? Totally awesome! I won't have to deal with the other witches, though I will miss Halia and Sebastian. Maybe I can get them cast on my show? I mean, every *Savvy* teen needs a best friend and a love interest. We will have the best time ever shooting. I can't believe that I was worried about getting fired! Now, I'm set for three more seasons though they probably would sign me for one hundred if they knew that I was immortal and will look like this forever.

But I am determined to go to college whether *Savvy* likes it or not. Real college, too. Not an online program that the other celebrities do so they can still be on the set every day. I dream of being able to spend all my time reading books. I can't even imagine ruining college by always having to hop on the next plane for auditions.

"Get back to the lesson before I change my mind." I want to hug him again, but he's already striding away.

Halia gives me a questioning look, but I just smile and give her a wink. Now isn't the time to talk about it.

We work on natural turns while a reporter from *Teen Glam* sets up a segment about my party. While they are fixing her makeup, I glance over and read her teleprompter. "We're here live at Ria's Quince rehearsal. But the big question on everyone's mind is, did sixteen-year-old Dulce have plastic surgery to save her role on the hit series *The Coven*? An insider on the set says yes."

¡Ay, Dios Mío! I'm the laughing stock of the entertainment industry.

Everyone thinks I'm like that stupid reality starlet that had like fifty procedures in a day.

My freak out is interrupted when Eva barges in the door. She beelines straight for me.

"So, after all I've done for you, you had me fired Dulce? How could you?"

Uh oh. I flee the dance floor, and she runs after me.

She corners me behind one of my aunt's gaudy garden sculptures. "Answer me!"

"I don't know what you're talking about. I never told anyone to fire you."

"I was told not to come to set today because you didn't need hair and makeup anymore. This is my job, Dulce. My life. Who did you hire to replace me? Who?"

Her face is red, and my heart breaks for her. But I can't tell her the truth. Not here, not now. And she wouldn't believe me.

I have to choose. And at this moment, I choose me.

"I'm sorry, Eva. I don't know what you are talking about. But since you no longer are employed by Savvy, I must ask you to leave."

Her jaw drops, and she throws up her hands. "Fine, Dulce. Fine. And don't you think for a second I don't know what's really going on with you."

She storms out of my house. A horrible thought crosses my head. *She's on to me. And if she's on to me, she must be eliminated.*

Gosh, what is wrong with me? I squelch that thought, attempt to lock down my emotions, and return to the dance floor when I hear a screech and the sound of metal crinkling.

Oh my god no!

I run inside my house and look out the window to the driveway. Eva's car has crashed into Padre Arturo's car. Smoke is billowing from the engine.

"Call 911!" someone screams.

I stand there transfixed at the window. Did I cause this crash from my evil thoughts? The curse is one thing, but can my fleeting desires, however evil, actually come true?

By now, the entire cast and crew have surrounded the cars. I hear sirens in the distance.

Please, dear lord, let them be okay. I know not what I have done. I don't move until the paramedics come ten minutes later.

I run to my room and collapse onto my bed, tears streaming down my face.

Five minutes later, I hear the sound of Sebastian's footsteps echoing through the hallway. "Duls, you okay?"

I turn to him. "No! Did you see what just happened? That's my fault! I caused that. I wished something bad to happen to Eva, and it did! And I'm sure Padre Arturo would've seen me and started an exorcism. I willed that too!"

"What? No, you didn't. It was an accident. Everything will be fine. The paramedics say they are both fine but are taking them to the hospital."

"Yes, I did. Sebastian, I'm sorry. I can't be with you. No matter how much I want to. I'll only hurt you."

His face hardens. "I can take care of myself. I want you, Dulce. And you want me. Stop changing your mind."

"I'm not changing my mind. I want you, too. But I'm dangerous. You don't get it."

"Actually, I do. We can get through anything together. I can help you break the curse."

I pause. I'm not sure I want to break the curse. I'm not sure what to say. After an awkward silence, he pulls me into him. "I hear you got offered a new contract?"

"Yeah."

His lips widen into a smile. "That's good news."

"Yeah. But everyone thinks I'm such a loser. Like I'm a vain teenager that destroyed my body with plastic surgery. I'm a total train wreck."

"No, you're not. Everyone's just jealous of you."

I shut the door and open the top drawer of my dresser. Inside contains a small box that holds a woven leather bracelet.

"Here, I want you to have it. This was my father's. He was a Marine, and he always protected me."

Sebastian slips on the bracelet. "I'd be honored. Thank you."

He wraps me against his chest. Losing my father at age ten was the most painful experience I had ever had. And I never even got to know my mother. I didn't want to lose Sebastian.

He kisses me and presses his body against mine on my bed. I kiss him back, losing myself in the moment but pull away from him, remembering that there are camera crews outside.

Sebastian holds me for a few minutes.

I break the silence. "We should probably get back."

"Yeah. Mr. Mulberg will start searching for us."

I roll out of bed and grab my rosary from my nightstand. Kneeling by my bed, I began to pray.

THE JEALOUSY

*I worshipped you. I grew **jealous** of every one to whom you spoke. I wanted to have you all to myself. I was only happy when I was with you.*

— OSCAR WILDE, THE PICTURE OF DORIAN GRAY

CHAPTER 12

Luckily Eva and Padre Arturo are fine. Just a few bumps and bruises. But my guilt remains. I still believe my thoughts caused the accident.

Sebastian picks me up the next morning, and we drive down Tiburon Boulevard, passed Blackie's Pasture, hit the U.S. Route 101 freeway, and pull into Mill Valley's Buckeye Roadhouse.

Brunch! Yum!

The valet takes his truck and Sebastian slings a duffle bag over his shoulder.

"This is a working brunch."

I have no idea what he has planned, but I couldn't care less. I'm just happy to be with him. And I'm beyond hungry.

We sit in a cozy booth, and I take a moment to appreciate the rustic décor. A fish sculpture hangs above the stone fireplace. I look out the window and marvel at the colorful fall foliage. A staircase leads to another dining room above us. This place feels like home to me, especially with Sebastian besides me.

I order the hot beignets with powdered sugar, coffee crème anglaise, and homemade jam. Sebastian orders the huevos rancheros—a safe choice, but still one of my favorites.

"So, I've been doing some research." Sebastian starts pulling items from the bag—a highlighted *The Picture of Dorian Gray*, a *The Wiccan Witch Inside You*, and more curiously, an odd, yellowing book that bore the title, *Curanderas in America*.

I thumb through its ripped pages. "What's this?"

He glances at what I'm holding and then goes back to digging in the bag beside him. "Nothing. Just some weird book my mom had on her coffee table. I grabbed it on the way out the door."

"Why did you grab it?"

He finally turns to me and pulls the book from my hand, setting it gently on the table. "No reason. Anyway, so I was reading Dorian Gray, and you're right. You're screwed."

Well, at least he spent some time away from studying his lines. "You read the entire book? In a day? It's long and kind of challenging."

He laughs. "Of course not. I skimmed it. But I did watch the Blu-ray. My mom loves Colin Firth, so she already had a copy." He winks at me. "So, you going to turn into a nympho?"

I wrinkle my nose. "You wish."

Sebastian knows I have never been with anyone. Halia and I are the only cast members that still have our V cards. I'm not a prude or anything, but I want my first time to be . . . I don't know, special.

Sebastian's eyes twinkle. "Hey. All I know is that last week you wouldn't touch me with a ten-foot pole and the other night you were all over me."

"It's not like that, and you know it."

"Yeah. I'm just playing."

The waiter brings us our food. As I begin to stuff my face, I notice that a young man seated upstairs seems to be staring at me. I adjust my view to get a better look, but when I glance again, no one is there.

I tug on Sebastian's sleeve. "Hey, did you see that guy upstairs?"

Sebastian glances toward the tables. "Which guy?"

"There was a guy up there. Now he's gone. I think he was staring at me."

Sebastian shakes his head. "I think you're paranoid. If he was looking at you, he was just staring because I have the most beautiful girl in here."

I smile and plant a kiss on his cheek. Sebastian is so sweet. "You really think I'm screwed?"

"Honestly, yes. But I have a plan. You said this happened after you said the everlasting youth spell on set. In the script coming up in a few weeks, there's a spell reversal with the girls. Just make sure to say it over the anthology, and it should just lift." Sebastian reaches over the table and takes my hand.

I exhale. He doesn't get it. I'm not ready to go back to my original self. Not just yet. "I guess."

"What? You sound like you're not happy about this news. Breaking the spell, Duls. Good thing."

"Yeah, I know it is. I know. But they offered me a new contract, Bas. Three years. And you and me . . ." How is he going to like seeing the old me all the time again now that he's gotten used to pretty me? "What if, like, I don't want to break the spell?"

His grip tightens on my hand. "Unh-uh, no. Don't do this, Duls.

Don't get like that. According to the book, you're going to do a ton of evil things, and the picture is going to get all mangled. Then you're going to have to leave all of your friends and family behind because you won't age and everyone will figure out your secret. One day you'll get so upset, you're going to stab the picture and die. How is turning into an evil bitch and then possibly dying cool?"

"I just won't do mean things and won't stab my picture, and I'll be fine." I take my hand back. "Anyway, Dorian said that the part about destroying his picture is fiction."

Sebastian rolls his eyes.

"How do you explain Dorian, then?" I challenge. "He's alive and sane."

Sebastian douses his eggs with Cholula sauce. "Dorian's a freak. A total stalker, Duls. I can't even believe you fell for his crap. My cousin hasn't found anything out about him yet, but he's still looking. I mean, the guy probably escaped from an asylum or just got out of jail."

"I thought you believed he was the real Dorian Gray. You even read the book, oh no wait, I mean watched the movie."

He shoots me an annoyed glare. "I watched the movie to see what kind of guy this Dorian is trying to be. But the guy you have met, I'm pretty sure he's a psychopath."

My blood boils. "Why are you so jealous of him? I'm with you. And you didn't even want to be with me until this spell." I wait for an angry reaction from him, but he just shakes his head.

"You can't be serious. I've always liked you. You were the one who was too insecure to get with me. I'm not jealous of Dorian."

I could feel my heart beat rapidly. I owe it to him to hear his plot out. "Fine. Sorry. I'm just testy." I force myself to calm down. "So that's it huh? Just say the reversal, and it should be done. You think it's that easy?"

"It has to be. You told me exactly what you did. So, we'll just break the spell, and this will all be over."

I take a sip of my hot mocha. "There is a spell reversal in the script, but it isn't to break the everlasting youth spell. It's for breaking a love spell. What am I gonna tell the girls? They aren't just going to gather around and say a spell that isn't in the script."

"I got that figured out. Just mess up your lines. You won't have to tell them anything."

"Whatever. You think Mulberg won't notice that I said the wrong spell?"

"It's a rehearsal. And I'll distract Mulberg. Just trust me."

Wow. He's going through so much trouble for me. I reluctantly nod my head in agreement. "Fine, I'll do it." Sebastian is right. This is for the best. I still believe I'm responsible for Eva and Padre Arturo's accident. It's the right thing to do to break the curse if it's possible. And at least I'll get to live like this for a few more weeks and reap the benefits.

It won't matter if I'm not spellbound anymore after I sign the contract tonight, so it's at least worth a shot.

We finish our brunch and talk about our future together. Words I have always been afraid of speaking. We decide not to come out to the press just yet and that when the time is right, we can do a joint interview and photo shoot together, so the paparazzi won't endanger our lives trying to get our first picture kissing. I close my eyes and hope, *pray* that everything will go exactly as Sebastian has planned.

My phone vibrates, and I pull it from my purse to find a text waiting for me.

Dorian: His plan won't work. Don't you think I've already tried everything?

My hand shakes, and I drop my phone. How the hell does he know about Sebastian's plan? Is he spying on him? On me? Is he here?

I quickly scan the restaurant for Dorian, but I don't see him. Then I remember that guy I saw earlier. I swear he had been watching me. Maybe he was some sort of spy . . .

Sebastian has pretty much dismissed Dorian as some stalker, not the real Dorian Gray. Rationally, Sebastian makes sense. But something in my heart tells me that Dorian is who he said he is. And if he is—I will never be free.

THE SKEPTIC

Skepticism is the beginning of faith.

— OSCAR WILDE, THE PICTURE OF DORIAN GRAY

CHAPTER 13

We arrive at Muir Woods for the day's shoot. This is my favorite place in the world, surrounded by the towering Redwoods, tanoak trees, ferns, while the stellar jays fly overhead.

Sebastian walks into my trailer to help me gather the items I need for the reversal. "It's showtime, babe. The girls are waiting outside."

I signed the contract this morning, and I have promised Sebastian that I will try to reverse the spell, even though I still have mixed feelings. It's a blast being the *it* girl of the season, but I can't shake the Internet rumors or the feeling that I am somehow doomed.

I rummage around the trailer and gather the ingredients: a pearl, black cloth, and string. Mama's rosary lays in my purse. I figure that by cutting the pearl off and using it in the spell, it will do more good for me now than saying a whole bunch of Hail Marys. As long as I remember to fix it before Maria finds out, I'll be good. I don't know what would make her madder—turning into a picture or damaging Mama's rosary.

I say a quick Hail Mary over my now broken rosary just for extra good luck. In a few minutes will I be back to my normal blotchy self?

Sebastian takes my hand, and we leave the trailer. The sunlight peeks through the forest, almost beckoning me to head toward the brightness.

Halia runs to my side. "So, how's your new boyfriend? Oh my God, Duls. I can't believe you two finally hooked up. It was only a matter of time. Though, if I were you, I'd have chosen Dorian. Did you see the death threats the Covettes are giving you on Twitter?"

Death threats? I haven't glanced at my twitter in days. My only worry has been figuring out how to navigate this curse. I place my finger over Halia's lips in a shushing sign. "We're not officially together just yet. We're working out some, um, things."

She shrugs. "I don't get you, girl. You've wanted him forever, and now you are taking your time?"

I don't respond since I'm not sure what to say. We walk over to the rest of the girls. "Guys, can we practice the spell breaking scene."

"Why? It's super short and easy," Vikki says as she gives me a side-ways look.

"I'm just super tired and didn't get a chance to run lines last night. Please?"

Asha stands and brushes some morning dew off her costume. "Fine, whatever."

I let Winter out of his cage and place him on the floor. I take a white candle from my cloak and light it. We hold hands across the circle as Sebastian looks on from the sidelines.

"I cast a spell asking for everlasting youth,

I now ask the favor of having the spell removed.

I understand to take back a spell means giving up something of my own to show my spirit is true and my intentions are good,

I give this pearl from a necklace I own.

I transfer the spell into the pearl and render the spell dormant.

No harm may come from the cancellation of this spell.

No further power shall it have.

This is my will—so be it."

I place the pearl and the cilantro into the cloth and wind it up with the string. After I tighten the final knot, I drizzle some candle wax on it. Now, I just have to get rid of it. I pull my arm back and throw the pouch as far as I can into the woods.

But I feel no surge of energy. No rush of adrenaline. Nothing. The spell hasn't worked.

Marcilla glares at me. "You screwed up your lines. You never mess up your lines."

"I did?" I raise my voice and act as if I am confused.

"Yeah, your line about the spell. You said for everlasting youth. That was a month ago. The script says for love lost. Just don't make a mistake when we shoot. I have a date tonight, and I don't want to be stuck all day doing reshoots because you flub your line."

"Thanks, Marci. I won't."

I motion to Sebastian. "I don't feel any different." I take a deep breath, and we walk toward where the pouch landed so I can get my Mama's pearl.

"It probably takes a while to work. I'm sure it reversed."

But I know nothing has changed. The everlasting youth spell worked immediately, and more importantly, I'd felt the original spell take hold of my body. I barely needed any convincing—my soul had been sure of it. "Maybe. After today's scenes, we can check. You can maim me or something and see if I recover."

"That won't be necessary," Dorian says from behind us, causing both Sebastian and I to turn. "You must be Sebastian, I presume. Dorian Gray. Pleased to make your acquaintance." He extends his pale hand to Sebastian.

Sebastian keeps his hand in his pocket, refusing to touch Dorian.

"Dorian, or whatever your name is, we have it all handled here. I'm taking care of Dulce from now on. You can go back from wherever it is you came from. London, a book, jail, an insane asylum."

Dorian laughs. "Amusing. But really, Sebastian, I'll be doing nothing of the sort. You see, your brilliant little spell reversal didn't work. Dulce brought this curse upon herself. It wasn't from the spell or from my novel being included in the anthology."

I pull my hair and scrunch up my face. "How did I bring this on myself? I simply lost a prop and used the anthology as a stand-in. I had no idea this could ever possibly happen. You act like I willed it."

A long smile stretches across Dorian's face. "You wondered what it would be like to look like that photo forever. You offered up your soul. And your wish came true."

The blood rushes through my face. I had wished that. And I meant it with all my heart when I uttered that damn wish.

Sebastian shoves Dorian, ripping the collar of Dorian's polo shirt. "Get out of here freakshow, or I'll call security."

Dorian straightens his clothes. "I'll leave. Dulce, you have my number. Call me when you need me, which will be soon. Cheerio." He pushes his sunglasses back on his head, twirls his keys, and walks toward the parking lot.

I slump against a nearby tree. A tear escapes down my cheek but dries almost instantly, despite the mist in the air. The silence stretches between Sebastian and me, and I can't bring myself to look at him.

"Sorry I pushed him, but he's no good. There's something off about that guy."

I look up at Sebastian. He is such a great guy and doesn't deserve to be dealing with my problems. "Sebastian, I just know the reversal didn't work. I feel the same as I did this morning."

Sebastian's eyes move over every inch of my face. I know he is searching for differences, differences he won't find. "Okay fine. It didn't work. I mean there were a lot of variables that weren't the same. We're in Muir Woods, not Mt. Tam. The spell was a practice, not a shoot. And wasn't that the *Dia de los Muertos* episode?"

"Yeah. But what does that have to do with it."

His eyebrows dance. "Don't you see? This is beyond Wicca. You must've tapped into something else. Magic—real Aztec Black Magic."

A breath escapes my lips. I don't believe in that stuff. Well, I didn't before. Wicca seems, well . . . harmless. Even beautiful—celebrating the Goddess and Mother Earth. I never feel guilty or like I am a bad Catholic playing a Wiccan Priestess, even though I still believe in the holy trinity. But what Sebastian is suggesting is something sinful. I don't want even to consider screwing around with black magic.

"Nuh uh. No way. Forget it. I'm not even going to go there. Are you serious? Are you talking about Black Magick and Sorcery?"

"No, of course not. My mom's a curandera. A healer. She's super Catholic. There's nothing Satanic about her healing. I'm sure she can help you break this. But if she can't fix this, we need to keep our options open. You have to trust me."

I do trust Sebastian, but I don't want to play around with real magic. But for the first time since the spell happened, I am getting really terrified. This is not right.

I lean into Sebastian. "I can't deal with this now. Halia says I'm getting death threats from your fans on Twitter. This is all too crazy. Let's just take a step back before I start becoming a Satan worshipper and you decide to make a virgin sacrifice out of me."

He breaks off a tree branch and throws it down. "Is this a joke to you? Fine. Whatever you say. But Duls, this is not good. At all. Something bad is going to happen. I can feel it. And if it does, I'm not going to wait for your permission. I'm going to do what I have to do."

I stare into his dark brown eyes. "Okay." But I know that Dorian isn't going to go away, and I'm not exactly sure that I want him to.

Sebastian puts his arm around me and leads me into the towering forest.

THE REALITY

*I believed in everything. The common people who acted with me seemed to me to be godlike. The painted scenes were my world. I knew nothing but shadows, and I thought them real. You came -- oh, my beautiful love! -- and you freed my soul from prison. You taught me what **reality** really is. To-night, for the first time in my life, I saw through the hollowness, the sham, the silliness of the empty pageant in which I had always played.*

— OSCAR WILDE, THE PICTURE OF DORIAN GRAY

CHAPTER 14

I t is the closing night of Romeo and Juliet. I can't wait to see
Sebastian play Romeo again and woo fair Juliet.

I want to show off his talent to everyone. I've invited everyone
I know to see him perform: Maria, Rosa, all the girls. We all sit in
the front rows of the theater with Sebastian's family.

I even texted Dorian. I want him to see Sebastian slay this role, so
Dorian will know that history doesn't repeat itself. Sebastian is
nothing like Sybil.

I address my friends. "Thanks for coming tonight. I'm so happy you
can all watch Sebastian in his element. When I first saw him
perform last week, I was completely in awe. This is where he comes
alive. When he speaks his first words, you will forget the world
around you. Sebastian is brilliant."

Marcilla rolls her eyes at me. "Dulce, you're such a weirdo. A week
ago, you pretended that you weren't into him and now you're acting
like his publicist. Relax, it's just a high school play."

I ignore her and sit in my seat. She isn't going to put a damper on his show.

Halia clutches my hand. "I think it's so cute how into him you are."

"Thanks, Halia. I'm so glad you understand me. I don't care what anyone thinks. Sebastian is amazing in this play, and I'm so happy we're together now."

The curtains pull back, and the play begins. They are at the Capulet's house, and Sebastian walks in with Mercutio and his friends.

His lips part and he speaks.

"If I profane with my unworthiest hand

This holy shrine, the gentle fine is this:

My lips, two blushing pilgrims, ready stand

To smooth that rough touch with a tender kiss."

But unlike last time, there is no emotion in his voice. It is surprisingly flat, almost lifeless. He looks dazed, and his words sound almost robotic.

I glance around the room, feeling my skin ice. Why is he embarrassing himself?

Maybe he isn't feeling well. I hang on his every word, but there is no improvement.

Halia whispers into my ear, "What's going on with him? He totally sucks."

I don't answer because I don't have an answer.

The next act begins, and I hold my breath, not looking forward to his monologue.

"But soft, what light through yonder window breaks?

It is the east and Juliet is the sun!"

One of the most famous scenes in Shakespeare is made a mockery of by Sebastian. He says those lines with no more passion than if he had been hocking ice cream. What is wrong with him? The audience is just as annoyed as I am, and they start talking amongst themselves. I can't take it anymore and slide from my seat and out of the theater. I wait outside the stage door until the act is over.

Fifteen minutes later, a few cast members come outside and light cigarettes. I ask one of them if they can get Sebastian.

He appears at the side door. "Hey, babe. Rough crowd tonight. Man, I totally blew it!"

I don't even want to look at him. "I'll say. Are you sick? You were brilliant in the last show I saw. Was there something wrong with the cues or the lighting?"

Sebastian grins at me as if his horrible acting is some kind of joke. "Nah, they're great. It's just . . . I don't care as much about acting. It was my world—something to occupy myself with since I had nothing to do up here. All my friends are in Los Angeles. It's just my mom and me up here, and you know how she is. I just threw myself into the craft. But now that I have you and we're together, I feel the world has opened up for me. For us. There is so much more to this life. I want to be with you."

My shoulders drop. This beauty, his art, his words, were what made me fall in love with him in the first place. Without all that depth, he is just another pretty face. "I thought you dreamed of getting an Oscar. Seeing you act the other night made me fall hard for you."

Sebastian crinkles his face. "You only like me because you thought I was good in the play? That's the stupidest thing I ever heard."

"It's not stupid at all. I respect and admire you. You are the only one of the cast that has a true passion for acting—the same passion I have for literature."

I hate to admit it, but Maria is right. Sebastian is common and boring. Not worldly like Dorian. What would my life be like if I end up with Sebastian? Some former child star turned real Hollywood housewife desperate to reclaim her childhood fame? The most I can hope for is to end up on some pathetic reality television show.

But with Dorian the possibilities are endless. We can travel, read, study, immerse ourselves in different cultures. Forever.

Maybe, I made the wrong choice.

Maybe, I should be with Dorian.

Sebastian's face blushes, and he closes his fist. "I've been bending over backward defending you to all these people, coming up with a plan to break the spell and this is how you repay me? You are acting like a spoiled brat, Dulce."

I look down at my feet. "Timing isn't right. This curse is my problem, not yours. I think, maybe, we should just take a step back so I can figure stuff out."

"Are you serious? I'm racking my brain on how to fix this so we can be together and you are dumping me? You need me right now. What are you going to do—run to Dorian?"

"I'm still shaken up after what happened to Eva and Padre Arturo. You can think I'm crazy, but Dorian is the only one who understands me. I don't want to ruin your life by my mistake."

Sebastian slams his fist into the door. "Fine, Dulce. You want to hang out with that freak? Who am I to stop you? But I won't be waiting for you when he breaks your heart."

He takes off the bracelet I gave him, tosses it to the ground, and then walks back into the theater.

Nausea fills my stomach. What have I just done? I've always liked Sebastian, always. I thought he never liked me, but it seems like I had been too insecure to give him a chance. Now I've ruined everything.

I drop to the floor and retrieve my father's bracelet.

I'm still there, wondering if I made the right choice when Dorian's hand lands on my shoulder. "Are you ready now?"

I have no choice. I have ruined my chances with Sebastian. I'm a danger to my friends. I must go.

"Absolutely."

Dorian puts his arm around my shoulders and leads me to his car. I take a final glance back at my high school, knowing that I'm leaving my life and my love behind.

THE TEMPTATION

*The only way to get rid of a **temptation** is to yield to it.*

— OSCAR WILDE, THE PICTURE OF DORIAN GRAY

CHAPTER 15

Dorian takes me to his place in Sausalito, which has a fantastic view of the Golden Gate Bridge.

Guilt still eats me up about Sebastian. I completely over-reacted about his acting. I was petty and selfish.

But it was for the best. I'm a danger to him.

I don't feel like I have a choice. Dorian is right. I can only hurt Sebastian. He could've been my soulmate, but with this curse, a curse I know I have, I can only be with one man. That man is Dorian.

If you love someone, let them go. I have to let Sebastian go.

And a part of me wants Dorian. I'm sick of being the good responsible girl, supporting my family, studying when my cast mates are out partying.

It's my turn to live. Explore. Indulge.

I think Dorian will lead me straight into his bedroom. Imagining his experienced hands caressing me makes my insides tingle. I straighten my clothes and twirl my hair.

Dorian senses my uneasiness. "Relax. I'm not a vampire. I don't bite unless you want me to."

I let out a nervous laugh and Dorian goes to the kitchen. Pots and pans rattle.

I perch myself up on a bar stool and gaze out at the bay, focusing on the quirky houseboats. "Are you a chef? I appreciate the seduction scene, but it's really not necessary. I want to be here. With you."

He whisks something together in a bowl. "I appreciate fine dining and good wine. You will, too. I'm in no rush to woo you, Dulce. We have all the time in the world."

I explore the apartment, searching for his picture, but come up empty-handed. Eventually, I end up back in the kitchen with Dorian, who is busy blanching something.

"So, what are you making?"

Dorian brings out a feast. "Well, to start with, I made a lobster bisque, and then we will have a salad with hazelnuts and goat cheese. For the main course, I prepared petit filet mignon with a béarnaise sauce and asparagus. And for dessert, we will have a chocolate ganache."

Yum, except for the steak. I don't eat meat, but I don't want to rattle Dorian. I am going to play along with him for now and be the student he wants me to be.

"Dorian, I've been thinking . . ."

He pours me a glass of Paul Meyer Merlot. "Yes."

"Why me? Was I just in the right place at the right time? Had you been searching for someone to spend your life with? Would you just like anyone with this curse?"

Dorian swirls the liquid in his glass and takes a sip. "No, of course not Dulce. As I've said, I see myself in you. And, you are beautiful. It's been so lonely for me over the years, living in the shadows of reality, reinventing myself every few years. I don't want anyone else. I'm willing to commit to one person. To you. For eternity."

I take a deep breath and inhale a small sip of the wine, preparing myself for what I'm about to say. I'm ready to give myself to him completely. He's everything I have ever wanted. For once, I don't have to worry about paying the bills and getting a new contract. Dorian will take care of me. No one has ever taken care of me.

My hand reaches across the table, and I touch him. "Dorian. I want you."

He wastes no time. Standing up, he cradles my body and leads me to the bedroom. As excited as I was seconds ago, my gut clenches in nervousness. I've always dreamt that my first time would be with Sebastian. I truly love Sebastian, even though I know he is wrong for me. Well, that isn't true. I'm the one who is wrong for Sebastian. Am I making a big mistake?

Dorian pushes me down on the bed and slowly undresses me.

"You, my dear, are exquisite."

He nibbles on my ears, kisses the nape of my neck, cups my breasts. When I try to kiss him back, he just pushes me back on the bed and focuses on me.

"Dorian. I want to lose my virginity to you. Make love to me."

Dorian just grins and sits back. "Dulce, my love, there is no rush. Let's just take our time."

Is he rejecting me? "You don't want me? I thought . . ."

He places his fingers on my lips. "No, on the contrary. I drive myself mad thinking about you. But we must wait. Until we are married."

Married? The Bride of Dorian Gray? Sounds like a TV movie. "I want my first time to be special, but we don't need to be married."

He moves to the edge of the bed. "Yes. We do. Otherwise, I will not consider making love to you. If we make love, and it doesn't work out, I'll never forgive myself for ruining you."

"Ruining me? Um, it's not the nineteenth century anymore. I'd be just fine. You aren't the only man in the world."

His fists clench. "I'm the only man for you, Dulce. I destroyed Sibyl by making love to her when we were engaged. When we broke up, she poisoned herself. I can't risk losing you."

Man, this guy is still hung up on a girl from a century ago. He gazes longingly away, and I realize that even though he is immortal, his heart is still human.

And I also realize that there is no limit on time to get over someone. Dorian still loves Sibyl. I could love Sebastian forever, even if he's not mine.

I crawl up behind Dorian and wrap my legs around him. "Let's go away together. I've always wanted to visit Boston, and since I'm applying to Harvard, it can double as a college tour. Can you take me? Tonight?"

His lips turn into a devilish smile. "Of course, my love, we will leave in the morning." He laughs and throws me back down on the bed. We kiss until the sun comes up.

THE SIN

*You will always be fond of me. I represent to you all the **sins** you never had the courage to commit.*

— OSCAR WILDE, THE PICTURE OF DORIAN GRAY

CHAPTER 16

Though I've been to the east coast several times, usually visiting New York for press tours and the talk show junket, I've never been to Massachusetts. I know our trip will be short because I have to be back on set in a few days. I consider texting my aunt to tell her that I'm visiting Harvard, but I decide against it. I love being emancipated. I'm sure she suspects I'm with Dorian, but I doubt she even cares as long as my checks keep rolling in.

Dorian instructs the limo to take us to his walk-up in Cambridge. Young men row on the Charles River. The multi-colored leaves highlight the cobblestone streets on this crisp fall day. There is so much history and culture here, and I am eager to immerse myself in the New England landscape as we head to campus.

I take his arm. "When was the first time you came here?"

"Wilde toured here and always told me what a delightful city it was. The first opportunity I had, I made my way over here in the late 19th century. I fell in love with Cambridge. It has all the charm of London without the stuffiness."

As we approach the main gates of the campus, an intense desire to move here overtakes me. I can imagine myself studying here—sipping a latte in the quad, my dog, Salsa, frolicking on the lawn, taking strolls with Dorian under the antique lamplights. All my hard work and sacrifice in school will be worth it if I can reach this goal. And to hell with my contract—I'm sure Dorian could buy me out of it. Time to be selfish.

Dorian abruptly stops, as if he sees something or someone in the distance.

"Are you okay?"

"Of course, my dear. Would you mind waiting here for a moment? I believe I saw an old friend walk by. If I catch up to him, I'll be sure to introduce you."

"Sure. I'll just wait for you at the library."

He gives me a quick peck on the cheek, and I sit on the steps of Widener Library.

My eyes follow Dorian. He stops and embraces a thin man who appears to be around my age. He looks familiar, but I don't think I've ever met him on any of my trips to the east coast. I observe them carefully as they talk, but then, between one blink and the next, the man is gone.

I know I am tired and have had a long day with the flight, but I am sure about what I just saw. A twisting feeling settles into the pit of my stomach as I remember the day Sebastian and I had brunch at the Buckeye, and I suck in a sharp breath. Is that where I know that man from?

"Who was that?" I ask as Dorian extends his hand to help me up.

"Oh, an old friend. He sends his regards but has a meeting to run to. He'll meet us tomorrow for dinner."

"An *old* friend? He looked around your age, er, I mean no more than eighteen. How could he be an old friend? Is he immortal like you?"

His lips twitch. "I've known his family for many years' time. He's a freshman here."

"Dorian, you were talking to him for a second, and he completely vanished before my eyes."

A heavy hand clasps on my shoulder. "You're tired, Dulce. Your eyes are deceiving you. After we were done speaking, I believe he slipped behind a tree and headed off."

A few students walk by us. I give a slight smile to them just in case they recognize me. "No, Dorian. He vanished. Like, poof! Before my eyes. Completely gone. I'm not crazy. I know what I saw."

"You are mistaken. Let's just get some lunch, shall we?"

I feel nauseous. Something is terribly wrong, but I have no idea what. All I know is that I can't trust Dorian and need to get away from him without raising suspicion as soon as possible.

We have lunch at a cute little Vietnamese restaurant off the square. But the yummy pho and spring rolls do little to soothe my fears.

After we go browse some stores, we head back to his place.

"Dulce, I'm going to stop by the market to pick up a few things. I won't be long. Call me if you need anything."

"Sounds good. I'll take a bath and then lie down."

Dorian walks out of the room and shuts the door. I hear the key click, and I know that I'm alone and have to act fast.

I walk around his home. Where is his picture? I need to find it. I know he told me it was in Switzerland but that is clearly a lie. He has to keep it with him at all times as he told me to do. But we were just in Marin. Did he ship it? Carry it in a secret hidden luggage compartment on the plane? Is it somewhere on him? Where is it?

Maybe I can discover some clues to our curse if I see it. There are paintings on every wall, most of which I assume are originals. I don't think Dorian is the kind of guy who would settle for replicas.

Books fill the shelves, yet four golden-bound gothic classics catch my eye: *She: A History of Adventure* by H. Rider Haggard, *The Invisible Man* by H.G. Wells, *Frankenstein* by Mary Shelley, and *Carmilla* by J. Sheridan LeFanu. All of these books are in my anthology. Yet, his own book is strangely missing.

That man I saw today. Was he invisible? Like *The Invisible Man*?

What if . . .

I slide the book off the shelf and open the first page. I gasp when a small photo floats out.

It is of Halia!

OMG! Holy Molé!

Is Dorian involved in some kind of sick plot to turn my coven into, um I didn't know, sex slaves for Gothic superstars? Some kind of teen female version of *The League of Extraordinary Gentleman*! Halia for the Invisible Man, Marcilla for, of course, Carmilla! Asha for She and Vikki for Dr. Frankenstein.

I open the other books, and sure enough, I am correct. Marcilla's picture is in Carmilla, Asha's picture is in She, and Vikki's picture is in Frankenstein.

Though I'm not sure of his intent, I know this is bad news. This is no random curse. I have been targeted. Our coven has been targeted. But by who? Dorian? Or maybe someone else . . .

I can't blow my cover. I have to see this through, or we won't be safe. Why hadn't I listened to Sebastian?

I push the book back in place and then reach into my purse to grab my phone. I will call Sebastian; beg for forgiveness, and hopefully, he can help me.

I realize that I'd forgotten to turn on my phone after we exited the plane. No one has been in touch with me since last night.

My iPhone powers up for what seemed like an eternity. When it finally comes on, it is flooded with messages, but the first one is the only one I read.

Halia: Sebastian's overdosed! He's in the hospital.

My phone slips from my hand, the glass screen shattering into pieces.

Overdosed on what? Sure, I've seen him get high a few times. Most of the girls except Halia and me have tried drugs. But he isn't into anything crazy.

I click on the TMZ app.

"BREAKING NEWS: Sebastian Vasquez—OVERDOSE AT SEVENTEEN!

Sebastian "Bas" Vasquez, star of Savvy's hit series, The Coven, was found unresponsive at a friend's house in Larkspur, California.

His friend's mother found Vasquez unconscious. He was rushed to Marin General, where he is currently listed in critical condition.

His family released a statement following the news. 'We want to thank everyone for their prayers, love, and support during this difficult time for our family.'

Sources tell TMZ that Sebastian was distraught over his breakup with his girlfriend, fellow The Coven star, Dulce Garcia."

What if he dies? This is all my fault. I should never have broken up with him. I am across the country when I should be there with him.

I try to open the front door, but it's locked from the outside. What the hell?

I push and pull on the lock but no luck.

What if Dorian doesn't let me go and I am trapped here?

I don't want him to be suspicious that I am on to him. So, I leave a note.

Dorian,

Sebastian has overdosed. I tried to call you but couldn't get a hold of you. I'm heading to the airport to catch the next flight out of here. Sorry.

Love,

Dulce

I wedge open a window, throw my luggage out first, and then squeeze out after it. I don't have time to wait for a cab, so I hightail it to the T and take the red line to the blue line to the airport.

Sebastian needs me.

THE TRAGEDY

*Those who are faithful know only the trivial side of love; it is the faithless who know love's **tragedies.***

— OSCAR WILDE, THE PICTURE OF DORIAN GRAY

CHAPTER 17

I hop on the next flight and fly into SFO. Paparazzi swarm me when I walk out of the gate, but I keep my head down and push through them.

"Dulce, Dulce, how is Sebastian?"

"Miss Garcia, did you know Sebastian was doing heroin?"

My feet falter, but I still don't look up. Heroin? Is that what they are saying? No way will I believe that he would shoot up, but my blood chills nevertheless.

I walk out of the sprawling terminal and text Halia, letting her know I've landed.

The minute I step out the glass doors, her Audi screeches to the curb, and a flurry of flashes blind us as I dive into the car.

"Why on earth were you in Boston? That was a really shitty thing to do. Dump Sebastian and take off with Dorian! You are so selfish."

I already feel shitty enough. I don't need her ragging on me. "Whatever, Halia. You were totally encouraging me to hook up with Dorian, and now you are giving me a hard time?"

"I did tell you to date him at first. But you were dating Sebastian, and then dumped him at his play because he sucked. That's way harsh, Duls. It wasn't like he ruined our show—it was a stupid high school play. You should've seen him that night. He was so upset. Drinking and partying. And now, he's like on life support."

My chest heaves. "So, you're saying I'm the one who freaking made him do heroin? Halia, seriously? Sebastian is his own person. It may have been shitty for me to leave like that, but I'm back. And I didn't leave because we broke up. There was way more going on than the play. The new show and my spell."

Halia just speeds up. "Here you go on about the spell again. I know I said I believed you, but now I'm not so sure. I trusted you because I thought you were my best friend. Maybe you did get plastic surgery so you could get a new series. Your own series. You've been so selfish lately, only thinking about your contract and not the rest of the girls. Or Eva who got fired. And certainly not Sebastian."

I grind my teeth. Here I'd been wracking my brain on how to protect Halia and the girls from a most certain threat of Dorian and these Gothic superstars, and she's accusing me of being self-centered? "No wonder no one is offering YOU your own show. You're a coward and will always be mediocre. I'm a star, and you can't stand it."

Halia steps on the brakes and almost crashes into the back of a Toyota Prius on 19th Avenue. "I'm through with you, Dulce Garcia. You can take your crappy spin-off that will probably be canceled, and your super sexy weirdo boyfriend and leave me alone."

She starts driving again but keeps her gaze straight forward and angrily pumps the gas. I think she's going to drop me on the side of the road, and I can't say I'd blame her.

She pulls up to Marin General, and I open the door and hop out. She speeds away, without even looking back.

God, have I become a monster? I don't even recognize myself anymore, on the outside or the inside.

As long as Sebastian is all right, I know I can fix this. I just need to break this spell and get my old life back.

Sebastian's mom sees me in the lobby and scowls.

"How is he?" I barely get the words out before I become choked up with emotion.

"He's still unconscious."

I nod my head. I don't know what Sebastian had told her if anything about our fight.

"Can I see him? I'm so sorry. I didn't . . . I mean I never thought . . ."

She casts me a glare and answers me with a small nod. "Five minutes. That's all."

I swallow hard. "Thank you."

I enter the room and find Sebastian on the hospital bed with tubes in his nostrils and an IV in his arm. His heart rate monitor is steady, but he is still.

I kneel by his bedside. "Sebastian. I'm here. I'm so sorry, babe. I don't know what's wrong with me. I love you, I do. It's always been you and me. I will make you the happiest guy ever if you just come back to me."

I hold his hands and pray.

But he doesn't move.

Not a flinch, a blink, or a smile.

The tears start seeping from my eyes. Sebastian might not make it, Halia hates me, Dorian is a creep, and Maria only cares about money. I feel completely alone.

I've thrown away my life because I wanted to be prettier, look younger. On the outside I am beautiful, but on the inside, I am ugly. I take the picture out and hold back a scream.

My face is almost a grayish tone. My mouth has deep-seated lines around it. My eyes are dull, cold, and soulless.

I crumple my picture into a ball, wanting to shred it to pieces. But a sharp pain explodes in my chest, and I collapse to the ground. I gasp for breath as I reach for the picture. Mustering up my strength, I roll off the floor, grab my picture, and straighten it out. My breath returns to normal.

This must've been why Dorian wanted to hold my picture hostage. So he could control me. All he would have to do to the picture, would be to mangle it, rip it, fold it, and I would feel immense pain.

Or if he destroyed it, he could destroy me.

No matter what it takes, I will find a way to rebuild my life and break my curse.

Then the most horrifying noise I have ever heard fills the room.

One slow, long beep.

Sebastian is flatlining. "Help! I need help!" I scream, but the door is already being flung open.

Nurses and doctors race in, kicking me out of the room. Tears fall down my face. Sebastian is dying. I will never hear his voice again, see his dimples, tell him I'm sorry.

"1, 2, 3!" I hear them yell.

The attendants wheel him out of the room. Leaving me alone.

I take my Mama's broken rosary out from my purse and pray harder than I have ever prayed before. I vow to do everything possible to break the curse if only Sebastian pulls through.

THE BELIEF

*As for **believing** things, I can believe anything, provided that it is quite incredible.*

— OSCAR WILDE, THE PICTURE OF DORIAN GRAY

CHAPTER 18

S ebastian somehow made it through the night in the hospital but his condition hasn't changed, and he remains unresponsive.

His toxicology reports came back, and he had tested positive for roofies and had a high blood alcohol level. There is a full-scale investigation, but so far, the police haven't been able to determine who had slipped him the drug.

But I have my suspicions. Maybe Dorian found a creative way to get Sebastian out of the picture. Maybe even the invisible man?

Just when I begin to lose hope, I reach into my purse and take out the book on curanderas Sebastian had given me. There is a remedy for mal aire.

I walk into the lobby and find his mother. "Diana, can you help me perform the remedy for *mal aire?*"

She blinks back tears. "Dulce, I already tried, but it didn't work."

I touch her hand. "Can we try again? I haven't been trained like you, but, uh, I'm different."

Her brow lifts. "Different? How so?"

I lower my voice. "I've been cursed. I mean, I think I cursed myself. There was this book." I pause and realize I'm not making any sense at all. "Look, I can't explain it, but I think I have some powers. Please, let me try with you."

She nods. "I'm willing to try anything. And my son loves you very much. He was devastated when you left him. Maybe hearing your voice will bring him back."

"I love Sebastian. I do. I'm so sorry for everything. I haven't been myself lately."

Her lips purse into a smile. I'm sure she blames me for Sebastian's overdose.

She takes my hand and we entire Sebastian's hospital room before she closes the door.

"Watch, Dulce."

She guides me on how to prepare the remedy. She pulls out of her bag a large, flat stone and a grinding stone called a *mano*, then takes herbs including a Mexican tobacco called *punche mexicano*, a root called *ruda*, spices, and oils.

Placing the *ruda* and the tobacco leaves on the flat stone, she methodically pulverizes them with the *mano*. I study her every movement, wishing that one day if I can break my won spell, I can become a curandera like her. She adds ground cinnamon, nutmeg, and a dash of salt and grinds them together. After attaching a piece of a nylon stocking to the bowl, she sifts the ground herbs through it with her hand. The fine dust filters to the bottom of the bowl, and she removes the coarse material from the cloth, rubbing a few particles on her throat and she says a prayer.

"Holy Patroness of those in need, Saint Rita, so humble, pure and patient,

whose pleadings with thy Divine Spouse are irresistible, obtain for me from thy Crucified Christ my request to heal my son, Sebastian. Be kind to me, for the greater glory of God, and I promise to honor thee and to sing thy praises forever.

Oh glorious St. Rita, who didst miraculously participate in the sorrowful Passion of our Lord Jesus Christ, obtain for me the grace to suffer with resignation the troubles of this life, and protect me in all my needs. Amen."

Then she asks me to repeat the prayer.

I feel at ease and no longer fear her healing. I have been raised devoutly Catholic, but her prayer gives me the reassurance that I need that I folk healing isn't dabbling with dark powers.

I have already made a dark pact—I didn't need to tempt fate again.

After grinding and screening the powder once more, she rubs olive oil on Sebastian's forehead, swabs the mixture from the bowl with a cotton ball, and dabs it on his head.

Sebastian doesn't move, and my heart drops.

"Dulce, you have to believe. It takes time."

"Can I stay with him?"

Diana hugs me. "Yes, please do. But you need to believe."

She leaves the room. I curl up next to Sebastian in his bed.

"Bas, I love you."

His eyes blink hard, but he doesn't say anything.

I repeat the prayer over and over, stroking his arm, praying and most importantly, believing.

I take a quiet moment and really center myself. I believe in the power of prayer, no matter what the religion. I had uttered a foolish wish, and my desire and belief overtook my soul. I believe that

Sebastian can be healed. And if he can be healed, then I can be saved.

I doze off but am awakened by a noise.

"Dulce," Sebastian whispers.

"Nurse!" I scream as I press the call button and jump off the bed. "Diana, he's awake!"

THE EMOTION

*The advantage of the **emotions** is that they lead us astray, and the advantage of science is that it is not emotional.*

— OSCAR WILDE, THE PICTURE OF DORIAN GRAY

CHAPTER 19

Diana rushes into the room. A team of doctors is called, and the nurse begins taking Sebastian's vital signs. I'm kicked out of the room as they work on him.

But for the first time in a while, I have peace. I know he's going to make it. He said my name.

An hour later, Diana comes and gets me. "Dulce, he's okay. He told me about your curse."

I bite my trembling lip. "Yeah, it's true. Maybe you can do the *male aire* treatment on me, and I'll be fine."

She shakes her head. "No, I'm afraid that won't work. The *male aire* is for when someone has cursed you. From what my son says, you cursed yourself. I'm sorry Dulce. You can go see him now. He's asking about you."

Dammit. But I won't give up hope. Now that Sebastian is saved, I know that the two of us can come up with something. I stand up and nervously enter his room.

He smiles when he sees me and tears come to my eyes. I kiss Sebastian and vow never to leave his side again.

"Babe, what happened? I'm so sorry I was so awful. I never meant . . ."

Sebastian takes my hand and begins to speak softly. "I don't know what happened. Yeah, I was pissed, but I just got wasted with the boys. Someone must've slipped me something."

Slipped him something?

I squeeze his hand and give him another kiss. To my surprise, he kisses me back, his warm lips touching my cold ones.

"Sebastian, I love you. I do. I'm so sorry about what I said. It's always been you. Only you. I'm just not myself. This curse has turned me into a monster."

His hand cups my cheek. "I love you, too, babe. And I forgive you. But we need to do something. If you don't break that curse, we're all in danger. I don't trust Dorian."

"I don't either." I pause, hesitant to tell him about my trip to Boston. But he will probably read about it in the rags. I need to be honest. Starting right now.

"I . . . I went to Boston with Dorian."

His face turns to a grimace, but I force myself to continue.

"I know, I'm sorry. But remember that guy I thought I saw at Buckeye? I think I saw him there also. And, get this. I found all of the Coven girls' pictures in these books Dorian had. I think this entire curse goes beyond just me."

His eyes widen. "I only care about you right now. Your curse. You need to cut your picture. Delete it from Instagram. Rip the one you made the wish over."

My hands shake, and I hold back a cry. "But, I can die."

"How do you know that? Just from Dorian's book? But he himself said that was fiction. Wilde wrote that. We don't know that, Dulce. You could stab the picture, and you could be fine. Hell, he could stab his own picture and be fine. You don't know. We have to risk it."

"No, I can't. If I'm wrong, then I die. I could die!"

A somber look crosses his face. His silence needs no explaining.

I have to do this. Because this curse has robbed me of my life. I am dead inside. Sebastian almost died.

It's a risk I have to take.

"I'll think about it."

I kiss him on the cheek and tell him he needs to rest.

I walk out of the room and look at my phone and see a text from Dorian.

Dorian: I hope Sebastian is well. I'm spending a few days in Boston but will return on November 1 for your birthday.

My birthday is on Day of the Dead. The episode where I became bewitched was set to air on November 1. That is it! This will be my only chance to break the spell. Maybe if I stab my picture on Day of the Dead, I can somehow reverse my spell and not die.

I text him back.

Dulce: Cool. Have a great time in Boston. I loved it there, and can't wait to go back. Miss you and excited to see you soon.

I have a week to get my act together. Get Sebastian healthy enough. A week to get the girls in on my plan.

THE MASK

*It was his beauty that had ruined him, his beauty and the youth that he had prayed for. But for those two things, his life might have been free from stain. His beauty had been to him but a **mask**, his youth but a mockery. What was youth at best? A green, an unripe time, a time of shallow moods, and sickly thoughts. Why had he worn its livery? Youth had spoiled him.*

— OSCAR WILDE, THE PICTURE OF DORIAN GRAY

CHAPTER 20

Sebastian was finally discharged from the hospital, and we immediately went to work on my plan organizing a big birthday bash at the Day of the Dead Celebration in the Canal.

As I place the final Marigold down at the altar for my parents, I take a moment to appreciate the beauty of this holiday. So many people think that there is something dark about Day of the Dead, but it was created to celebrate our beloved.

I went all out this year. Handmade sugar skulls, fresh tamales that my aunt and I slaved over all night, a bottle of tequila, fresh sweet pan dulce, pumpkin seeds for the visiting spirits, candles and a skeleton dog who will guide the spirits to our land of the living.

And most importantly, framed pictures of my parents. One of their wedding picture, one of my father in his Marine uniform, and one of my mother at her high school graduation. I pause when I stare at her picture—she is only a year older than I am now. I resemble her so much. But as beautiful as she is in her picture, I notice for the first time that she isn't perfect either. Her nose had the bump that mine had on it before this spell, her skin wasn't translucent, and her hair was frizzy.

I don't want to be perfect anymore. I want to be beautifully imperfect. I want to look like my mom. I want to be me.

Sebastian places his hand on my shoulder. "You ready?"

I nod my head. "Yes.

He takes my hand and leads me over to the girls on my show. They all look stunning and are costumed to kill. Full on Day of the Dead makeup, sugar skulls, spider webs, and rhinestone adorn their faces. Surprisingly, they all decided to come. I wouldn't blame them if they hadn't after the way I'd treated them.

I hug Halia. "I'm so sorry, girl. I was way out of line. Please forgive me."

"Well, you're lucky it's your birthday. But I'm sick of perfect Dulce. I just want my friend back."

I push back her hair and whisper in her ear. "Well, you are about to."

She crinkles her face but doesn't question me.

I turn to the rest of the girls. "Thanks for coming to my party. Sorry for the way I've been behaving. I've been going through something."

Asha glares at me, and for a second, I think she's going to slap me. And I would deserve it. But instead, she embraces me. "We forgive you. And it's your birthday. What are we doing? Just party by your amazing altar? Wow, Duls, your mom was beautiful."

I smile. "Yes, she was. I have a favor to ask you. Will you say a spell with me?"

Vikki's face contorts, making her already gothic makeup look even more sinister. "Why? We aren't witches. We just play them on television."

"That's the thing. You have all been asking me about what happened to my face. I was cursed the night of the shoot when we said the youth spell." I pause, purposely leaving out the part about the anthology. Only Halia, Dorian, and Sebastian know about it. If I am lucky enough for this spell to reverse, I will burn the book and put an end to the madness forever. "I didn't want to tell you all because I didn't think you would believe me. I need your help."

Marci walks closer to me and studies my face. "Which spell? So that's why you screwed up your line the other day. You were trying to trick us into reversing your spell. I knew it!"

Adrenaline races inside me. Marci believed. If I could get the girls to believe, this would work. "Yes, I did. But that day, I didn't believe. And honestly, I didn't want it to work. I wanted to have this power. But now, I just want my old life back."

The girls surround me, and we hold hands in a circle. "The night of that shoot, I wished with my whole heart to look like my picture. And you girls are such great actresses—we created magic. We are witches. Please try this for me."

Halia's gaze focuses on the anthology in my hands. "I'm game."

I shift my stance, uncomfortable from her stare. Why do I think she's plotting something?

I can't worry about her now. I have to do this.

Sebastian walks over to me and hands me my athame and a pouch. I take a white candle from my cloak and light it. And like we did the other day at Muir woods, we hold hands, and I begin to speak.

But this time, I believe in what I'm saying.

And I want to go back to being me.

"I cast a spell asking for everlasting youth,

I now ask the favor of having the spell removed.

I understand to take back a spell means giving up something of my own to show my spirit is true and my intentions are good,

I give this pearl from a necklace I own.

I transfer the spell into the pearl and render the spell dormant.

No harm may come from the cancellation of this spell.

No further power shall it have.

This is my will—so be it."

My book is open to my picture and Dorian's book. My hand clutches my athame. Is this my last moment of living? Will I be committing suicide by stabbing my picture?

I take a deep breath and say a silent prayer. I believe the picture and the desire for perfection caused my curse. And I believe destroying it will free my soul.

I hesitate for a second, but one look at Sebastian and I know this is what I want. I plunge the blade into my picture.

Blood rushes through my body, and a surge of energy electrifies me. I feel hot and cold simultaneously, burning my skin but chilling my heart. A wave of pressure takes over my head. A scream escapes my lips, and I black out.

My head fills with more images, but for the first time since I was cursed, the images are uplifting. Sebastian and I dancing at prom. Sebastian and I throwing our caps off at graduation. Sebastian and I studying at college. Sebastian and I making love for the first time.

And in all my images, I'm no longer perfect. I'm just me. Just old Dulce. Unfiltered and free.

THE DREAM

*Her eyes caught the melody and echoed it in radiance, then closed for a moment, as though to hide their secret. When they opened, the mist of a **dream** had passed across them.*

— OSCAR WILDE, THE PICTURE OF DORIAN GRAY

CHAPTER 21

My eyes blink from the bright lights, and the first face I see is Sebastian's.

"Babe, babe, thank god you're awake."

The room slowly comes into focus. I'm back in the hospital.

Sebastian shoves a mirror in my face. "It worked, Dulce. You did it. It worked."

I stare at my reflection and see a big zit on my chin. I touch it to make sure it's real. I've never been happier to be broken out.

"Ay, Dios mío! We did it!"

Sebastian pulls me into a long kiss. But our intimate moment is interrupted.

The door flings open, Dorian standing in front of it.

Sebastian stands up, but I put out my hand to stop him.

Dorian's eyes focus on me. "What have you done, Dulce? Where's your picture?"

"I destroyed it."

"How could you? You could've killed yourself."

I motion for him to come closer to me. "But I didn't, Dorian. I'm still here. If you stab your own picture, you will be saved. Somehow you believed what Wilde wrote about your curse. But it's not true. Free yourself. Live one honest life. Show me your picture."

He takes a breath, long, pained. "I can't Dulce. It's grotesque."

"Sebastian, will you give us a moment?"

Sebastian shakes his head. "No, sorry. I'm not leaving you alone with him."

I scowl but appreciate the protectiveness. I lower my voice and touch Dorian's cold hand. "Show me your picture."

His hand shakes as he reaches into his wallet to take out a folded up, laminated square. He slowly opens it.

My jaw drops and I let out an audible gasp as study the most disgusting, withered, wrinkly, man in the portrait. The only resemblance to handsome Dorian is the amethyst eyes, though in this picture they are sinister.

Dorian looks away in shame.

"Sebastian, do you have my athame?"

"Yup." He hands me my blade, and I place it in Dorian's palm,

"Do it. Don't be scared."

Dorian touches my cheek. "If I die right now, I want you to know that I truly love you. You are special, Dulce." He turns to Sebastian. "You better treat her right, or you will regret it for the rest of your life."

"I plan to."

Dorian's fingers grasp the handle, and he stabs the picture viciously.

His body contorts, and he yelps in pain as if he's dying. Did I just kill him?

He crumples to the ground, and I leap out of bed.

"Dorian! Dorian!" I check his pulse and feel nothing. I press the hospital button.

A nurse rushes in and checks me. "It's not me. It's my friend. I think he's dying!"

A doctor is called as the nurse begins doing CPR. I pray again, pray for Dorian's soul, pray that he will have one shot to redo his life on his terms.

I hear a gasp for air, and it's the sweetest sound I hear.

"He's breathing!"

"Dulce!" Dorian yells out as the doctors lift him onto a gurney and take him away.

Sebastian kisses me. "You are so brave. I love you."

"I love you too."

EPILOGUE

DORIAN

Dulce Garcia is my angel. The first time I heard about her, I thought she had been cursed so I could find true immortal love. But now I know she was meant to break my curse and teach me how to live without fear. For years, I have been afraid of damaging my picture.

And now I'm free.

I've enrolled in high school, determined to live one lifetime with normalcy. Dulce has vowed to be my friend forever, and I have chosen to remain in Marin.

Maybe one day I will fall in love again. Finally start a family as I have always craved. But I'm going to savor every moment of my new life.

I was wrong when I said that Dulce owed me her soul. Instead, she has saved mine.

Halia Momoa

I stand in my trailer, pacing back and forth, biting my nails and trying to curb my anxiety. No matter how many times I shoot a scene, I still feel nauseous every time. You think as an actress, I'd get used to the cameras, the spotlights, and the intrusive media, but it never gets easier.

If only I could be invisible. I could date whoever I choose and wear whatever I fancied without worrying that my choices will end up on the front page of every tabloid.

"Halia, five minutes! And don't forget to bring *The Book of Shadows*."

I reach for the prop book, but then something catches my eye. Dulce's *Anthology of 19th Century Literature of the Supernatural and Science Fiction*.

I had grabbed it when she passed out after her birthday spell.

After all, it had worked. This book, combined with her belief had made our witchcraft work.

"Coming!" I yell back.

Two seconds to choose and my hand lands on the anthology. Dulce's spell had been easy enough to break.

After all, what is the harm in me trying a little magic?

Stay tuned for *The Disappearance of Halia Momoa*

Thank you for reading my book.

If you liked it, would you please consider leaving a review for The Picture of Dulce Garcia.

For the latest updates, release, and giveaways, subscribe to *Alana's newsletter*.

For all her available books, check out Alana's *website* or *Facebook page.*

Follow me on *Bookbub*.

ALSO BY ALANA ALBERTSON

Want more romance?

Love Navy SEALS?

Meet Erik! I'm a Navy SEAL, a Triton, a god of the sea.

And she will never be part of my world. *Triton*

Meet Pat! I had one chance to put on the cape and be her hero. *Invincible*

Meet Kyle! I'll never win MVP, never get a championship ring, but some heroes don't play games. *Invaluable*

Meet Grant! She wants to get wild? I will fulfill her every fantasy. *Conceit, Chronic, Crazed, Carnal, Crave, Consume, Covet*

Meet Shane! I'm America's cockiest badass. *Badass* (co-written with *Linda Barlow*)

Love Marines?

Meet Grady! With tattooed arms sculpted from carrying M-16s, this bad boy has girls begging from sea to shining sea to get a piece of his action.
Beast

Meet Bret! He was a real man—muscles sculpted from carrying weapons, not from practicing pilates. *Love Waltzes In*

Love Immortals?

My mad wish may cost me my soul. *The Picture of Dulce Garcia*

Who's haunting America's favorite ballet? *Snow Queen*

ABOUT THE AUTHOR

 ALANA ALBERTSON IS the former President of RWA's Contemporary Romance, Young Adult, and Chick Lit chapters. She holds a M.Ed. from Harvard and a BA in English from Stanford. A recovering professional ballroom dancer, she lives in San Diego, California, with her husband, two young sons, and five dogs. When she's not saving dogs from high kill shelters through her rescue Pugs N Roses, she can be found watching episodes of UnREAL, Homeland, or Dallas Cowboys Cheerleaders: Making the Team.

For more information:
www.authoralanaalbertson.com
alana@alanaalberton.com

ACKNOWLEDGMENTS

Wow. I've been writing Dulce Garcia for over ten years. I have so many people to thank.

I'd like to thank Deb Halverson for her initial edits.

M-E Girard for being Dulce's first beta.

Deb Nemeth for providing amazing insight to this book and convincing me to have Dulce end up with Sebastian.

Ashley Williams for your edits on this project.

Regina Wamba for doing the amazing cover.

Peggy Martinez for choosing Dulce to go in the Lit-Cube box.

SY and Maia from Radish for featuring Dulce on the app.

78123679R00131

Made in the USA
Columbia, SC
09 October 2017